THE TRAP

Contents

Foreword by Alistair Ian Blyth   5

The Trap   13
The Rag Doll   75

ME: An Unabridged Autobiographical Novel   195

THE TRAP

Two novellas by Ludovic Bruckstein

Translated from the Romanian by Alistair Ian Blyth

Foreword

Ludovic Bruckstein's *The Trap* and *The Rag Doll* are both set during the Holocaust, the first in Sighet, the second in a nameless town very much like it, both of them part of the unique Jewish and multi-ethnic milieu that developed over hundreds of years in the northern Carpathians and Transcarpathia, a geographic area encompassing Galicia, Ruthenia, Maramuresch and Bukowina, regions that lie within present-day Romania, Ukraine, Poland and Slovakia. The history of Sighet (Marmaroschsiget), situated on the border with the Ukraine in present-day Romania's Maramureș region, encapsulates both this lost multi-ethnic world and the twentieth-century catastrophes that were to destroy it: fascism and the Holocaust, followed by Red Army occupation and decades of totalitarian rule. Although it was once home to a thriving Jewish community, no more than a dozen Jews now live in Sighet, a town famous today for its prison, where, in the Stalinist period, inter-war democratic political leaders and other 'enemies of the people' met a brutal end and were buried in unmarked graves, and which is now a museum and Memorial to the Victims of Communism. At the turn of the twentieth century, the town, then part of the Austro-Hungarian Empire, was home to sizeable Hungarian, Romanian, German and Jewish communities. In 1920, following the Treaty of Trianon, the southern part of the Maramuresch region became part of Greater Romania, and twenty years later it was annexed to Hungary consequent to the Second Vienna Diktat. After the commencement of Operation Barbarossa and Germany's invasion of the Ukraine, the Horthy regime rounded up a part of Sighet's Jewish population in August 1941 and sent them in freight cars over the border to Kamienets-Podilskyi, where they were massacred along with Jews from the local ghetto and deportees from elsewhere in Hungary. In 1944, German forces occupied Hungary and, with the collaboration of local fascists, herded the Jews into ghettos. Over the course of a week in May 1944, the around thirteen thousand Jews who had been confined to the Sighet ghetto, under armed guard and enduring squalid, overcrowded conditions, were deported to Auschwitz on four trains of freight cars. The deportees included Elie Wiesel (1928–2016), who was to win the Nobel Peace Prize in 1986, and Yiddish and Romanian-language writer Ludovic Bruckstein (1920–1988).

Ludovic (Joseph-Leib) Bruckstein was born in Munkatsch (Mukachevo), a town in Ruthenia with a large Jewish population, some eighty miles north-west of Sighet, which during the disintegration of the Austro-Hungarian Empire became part of the newly established Czechoslovakia and then part of the Ukrainian Soviet Socialist Republic at the end of the Second World War. Like the Jewish population of Sighet, where the Bruckstein family moved after Ludovic was born, and of so many other similar towns across the region, the Jews of Munkatsch perished during the Holocaust, massacred by Einsatzgruppen or transported to the gas chambers of Auschwitz.

In Sighet, Mordechai Bruckstein, Ludovic's father, established a business, exporting locally picked medicinal herbs and producing walking canes in a small factory. Ludovic Bruckstein began to write fiction at an early age, thereby continuing a long family tradition of Hassidic storytelling, which he was later to describe in the short story 'The Destiny of Yaakov Maggid' (1973). A *maggid* is a traditional Jewish storyteller, who narrates stories from the Torah and, in the case of the Hassidic *maggidim*, hagiographic tales of the movement's founder, Israel ben Eliezer (1698–1760), or the Baal Shem Tov, which means "Master of the Good Name." Chaim-Josef

Bruckstein, Ludovic's great-grandfather, was an early Hassid, a follower of the Baal Shem Tov, and the author of a book titled *Tosafot Chaim* (*Life Glosses*). His grandfather, Israel Nathan Alter Bruckstein, was a Hassidic rabbi in Pystin', a town in Galicia, ninety miles northeast of Sighet, and wrote two books, *Emunat Israel* (*Faith in Israel*) and *Minchat Israel* (*Gift of Israel*).

As a young man, Ludovic Bruckstein was to experience at first-hand the increasing atmosphere of anti-Semitism in Greater Romania and the hostile environment for Jews systematically created by Romanian officialdom, which he evokes in the novella *The Rag Doll* (1973). Even before the outbreak of the Second World War and the implementation of the "Final Solution," Romania's Jews were subject to harsh persecution, including the kind of senseless, soul-destroying, draconian bureaucratic requirements described in *The Rag Doll*, whose calculated, malicious purpose was to make everyday life all but impossible for Jews. In 1937–38, the government of nationalist poet and anti-Semite Octavian Goga (1881–1938) passed race laws rivalled in their severity only by those of Nazi Germany, whose measures included stripping a quarter of a million Jews of their Romanian citizenship, making them citizens of nowhere. After war broke out and Romania, under the dictatorship of Marshal Ion Antonescu, allied itself with Nazi Germany, the hostile environment for Jews further degenerated into the open violence of organised pogroms, including the Jassy Pogrom of 29 June-6 July 1941, in which more than thirteen thousand were murdered—shot, beaten and hacked to death, crammed into sealed freight cars and left to die of thirst and suffocation. By this time, Maramureș, and with it Ludovic Bruckstein's home town of Sighet, was under the control of another Nazi ally and fascist regime, having been ceded to Admiral Horthy's Hungary by the Second Vienna Diktat.

Ludovic Bruckstein's novella *The Trap* (1988), which he completed shortly before his death from cancer, describes the reactions of the protagonist, Ernst, to the anti-Semitic measures introduced by the Nazis and the Horthy regime, such as the compulsory wearing of the yellow star. Ernst, a university student, is shocked by the utter absurdity of it: Ultimately, it is ridiculous to reduce an individual human being to a yellow patch emblazoned with a letter of the alphabet, in this case, the letter J. Why not make Catholics and Lutherans wear the letter C or L? Or, to push the absurdity to its limit, why not have doctors and barbers wear an armband bearing the letter D or B? It will turn out that the absurdity of labelling people, the language of hatred that reduces the individual to a type, is the first step toward dehumanising them, an inexorable process whose final step is necessarily their annihilation; official denial of the right to human individuality is preliminary to physical extermination.

After Sighet's Jewish men are rounded up on the night before the Sabbath and subjected to collective humiliation by the commanding officer of a newly arrived detachment of the SS, Ernst decides to escape the oppressive absurdity that now reigns in the town, taking refuge with a family of Romanian peasants in the hills. And it is from the hills above the town that he witnesses the progression from absurd humiliation to extermination, when Sighet's Jewish population is first confined to a ghetto and then transported by train to a destination unknown. At the end of the war, when Ernst comes out of hiding and descends once more to the town, he is promptly arrested by an officer of the Red Army – the representative of another regime that reduces individuals to labels and types: enemy of the people, kulak, bourgeois, rootless cosmopolitan, etc. – on the absurd grounds that an arrest quota has to be met, regardless of who is arrested. In other words, another dehumanising denial of human individuality. Ernst is herded into a freight car with the other prisoners who make up the quota and transported to the labour camps of Siberia.

Unlike Ernst and Hannah, the protagonist of *The Rag Doll*, Ludovic Bruckstein did not manage to elude the train to Auschwitz, but like them both, he was to lose almost his entire family to the gas chambers. Prisoner A37013, Ludovic Bruckstein escaped the gas chamber only because, as an able-bodied young man, he was transferred to forced-labour camps in Hildesheim, Hanover, Gross-Rosen, Wolfsberg and Wüstegiersdorff, where he was made to repair the damage to railway tracks caused by nightly Allied bombing. Liberated by the Red Army in May 1945, he made his way back to Sighet, where he edited a Yiddish newspaper, *Unzer Lebn* (*Our Life*) and wrote a highly successful play, *Nacht-Shicht* (*Night Shift*), which was performed in Yiddish theatres in Bucharest and Jassy from 1948 to 1958. The play tells the true story of the Sonderkommando revolt at Crematorium IV in the Auschwitz-Birkenau concentration camp, which took place in October 1944.

Ludovic Bruckstein went on to write twenty plays in both Yiddish and Romanian, including *The Grinvald Family* (1953), *The Return of Christopher Columbus* (1957), *An Unexpected Guest* (1959), *Land and Brothers* (1960), for which he was awarded the Prize of the Union of Writers and the Order of Labour, *An Unfinished Trial* (1962), and *As in Heaven, So on Earth* (1968). At the same time, he wrote short stories for the literary press, which were collected in the volume *Panopticum* (*The Wax Museum*) in 1969. The following year, he applied for an exit visa to emigrate to Israel, where his younger brother, the only other member of his family to survive the camps, had emigrated in 1947. In the year and a half before he was finally allowed to leave the Romanian Socialist Republic with his wife and son, he was forced to resign his job and found himself ostracised as a traitor to the communist regime.

Settling in Tel Aviv, Ludovic Bruckstein continued to write fiction, mostly in Romanian and sometimes in Yiddish, which, rather than Hebrew, were the first languages of émigrés from Romania. His short fiction, collected in the volumes *The Destiny of Yaakov Maggid* (1975), *Three Histories* (1977), *The Tinfoil Halo* (1979), *As in Heaven, So on Earth* (1981), *Perhaps Even Happiness* (1985), *The Murmur of the Waters* (1987), include both timeless parables, full of humour and Hassidic wisdom, and stories of the concentration camps, which, no matter how harrowing, always convey an abiding love of humanity, of the unique human individual that cannot be reduced to a label or type.

In communist Romania, however, the name Ludovic Bruckstein was erased from the official history of literature. Even after the fall of communism, his novels and short stories, written in Romanian, but published in Israel, are almost entirely unknown to readers in his native country. It is a paradoxical situation for so important a twentieth-century Romanian writer, but to read the powerful, symbolically charged novellas *The Trap* and *The Rag Doll* is to understand how it could not have been otherwise.

Alistair Ian Blyth

ALISTAIR IAN BLYTH is one of the most active translators working from Romanian to English today. A native of Sunderland, England, Blyth attended the universities of Cambridge and Durham, and has resided for many years in Bucharest. His many translations from Romanian include: *Little Fingers* by Filip Florian; *Our Circus Presents* by Lucian Dan Teodorovici; *Occurrence in the Immediate Unreality* by Max Blecher; and *Coming from an Off-Key Time* by Bogdan Suceavă. Blyth has previously translated *Life Begins on Friday* by Ioana Parvulescu for Istros Books.

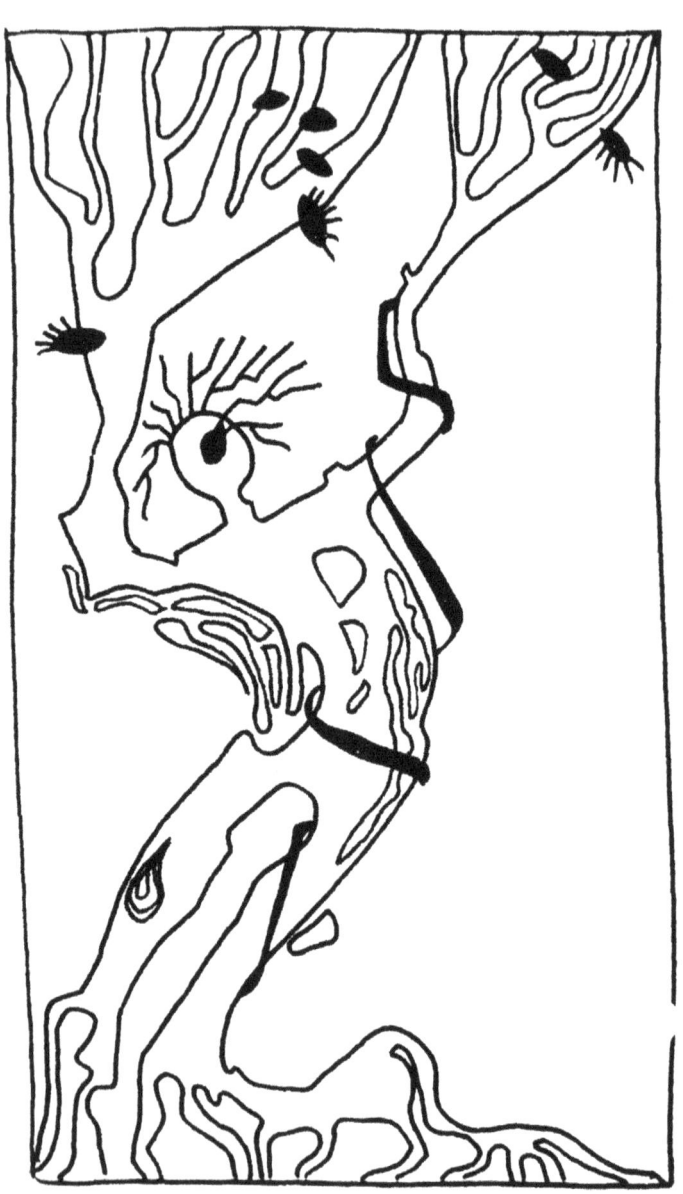

THE TRAP

1

The train crawled eastward, snaking along, black and sleepy. Inside the crowded goods wagon, with his knees to his mouth, Ernst listened to the monotonous clack-clack-clacking of the wheel beneath him. *'Halt! Stoi! – Halt! Stoi! – Halt! Stoi!'* the wheel seemed to say. And the steel of the other wheels in the other three corners of the wagon made muffled reply: *'Halt! Stoi!'* Stop! Stop! Stop!…

The train did not stop. Except rarely, on sidings, in deserted stations. And the doors did not open.

The war was over. 'What joy!' said Ernst to himself, sardonically. His anger had since evaporated. What else could he do except be angry, or not be angry? He could change nothing. Absolutely nothing… The lump in his throat had dissolved and now he felt like laughing. Yes, he felt like laughing, nothing less!… The wheels of the train clacked. He sank into a torpor. Inside the crowded goods wagon: the monotonous breathing of some sixty people, sitting like parcels on the plank floor, with their knees to their mouths. And a sour, stale stench of sweat. Among them was *that very same* young man in black uniform, a uniform now shabby, without epaulettes, without tabs. Or was he mistaken?… Nonetheless, the slicked chestnut hair was the same, the delicate profile was the same, the razor sharp nose, the greenish eyes were the same. He was yet to utter a word, but if he had opened his mouth, Ernst would have recognised that strident voice of his:

'*Halt!* Stop!'

At the time Ernst had worn a yellow star sewn on his back. And on his chest. At first he had been furious, outraged. And then depressed. Why that stigma? Merely because a man was of a different nation? Of different ethnic origins, as they put it… When timid, frightened creatures began to appear on the street, with yellow stars on their chests and backs, it became somehow comical.

From above, from the crests of the surrounding mountains, you could see the town in the valley, like an island between the waters of the Tisza and the Iza: the town of Sighet, not a very large town, but an important one, the county administrative seat; indeed, it had a courthouse and a large prison, five Christian churches: Catholic, Uniat, Orthodox, Reformed and Russian Orthodox; a few Protestant prayer and meeting houses; five synagogues and around thirty Jewish prayer houses; a large hospital with many wards; a mental asylum; six primary schools; four lyceums; a large café that served Turkish coffee and tea in the front salon and which had rooms for billiards and cards at the back; a hotel with twenty rooms on the upper storey, pretentiously named The Crown; two small cake shops on the Corso, which was the main street; a brothel at the edge of town, which was named the Jardin for some unknown reason, since there was no garden nearby, but only a yard at the back, rank with weeds; and a Palace of Culture in the select district, which, with its four turrets and massive wrought iron gate, imitated a mediaeval castle, in the late, grandiloquent style of the Austro-Hungarian Empire… It was from in front of the wrought iron gate that the strident command had rung out:
   '*Halt!* Stop!'

The train came to a sudden stop, its brakes screeching. Through the bars of the small window could be seen a patch of bluish sky. Inside, in the semi-darkness, the crowded, monotonously breathing bodies were barely distinguishable. From up ahead the locomotive gave a protracted whistle, and then the train set in motion, its metal creaking once more…

It had been Saturday and Ernst was hurrying to get home in time for lunch. He was determined to avoid tedious reproaches. All week he would eat sporadically, where and when he could, as his time allowed or his stomach demanded, but on Saturdays all the members of the family had to take their turn washing their hands in fresh water drawn from the well in the yard, they had to sit around the table, festively laid with a white damask cloth and gleaming crockery of glass and porcelain, all of them had to sit down together. His parents and the family tradition allowed no one to be late. And so Ernst was hurrying to get home in time for lunch, when all of a sudden he heard behind him a strident voice, like a military order:

'Halt!'

Ernst stopped. It was as if he could feel eyes boring into his back, into the spot where his yellow star was sewn. He turned around. The greenish eyes now lingered on the yellow star fixed to his chest, on the left, above his heart. In front of the wide-open wrought iron gate of the Palace of Culture, which Ernst had been passing, there stood a tall, brown-haired young man with a thin, razor-sharp nose, with small, greenish eyes, wearing a clean, immaculately tailored black uniform and highly polished boots.

'*Komm'her! Komm'her!* Come here!'

And since Ernst gazed at him rooted to the spot, bewildered by that rigid black apparition, by that cold, cutting voice – nobody had ever spoken to him in such a voice – and because he was in doubt as to whether he was really the person being spoken to, the officer yelled: *'Ja, ja! Du, herein!* Yes, yes! I'm talking to you! In here! In here!' And he pointed his arm at the vaulted entrance of the palace.

In that moment of surprise and confusion, Ernst did not realise that with that curt, cutting shout, that *'Halt!'*, that gesture inviting him inside the tall vaulted entrance of the Palace of Culture, the war had finally arrived in that quiet, peaceful little town hidden away in a valley of the Maramureş Mountains. He did not realise his life had entered a strange circle, a hallucinatory ring dance, which no sooner did it end but it would begin again in the same place and with the same curt, cutting shout, but spoken in a different tongue…

Indeed, till that shouted *'Halt!'* the wind of war had blown but lightly, over the radio airwaves that brought news of battles and advances and retreats in faraway, unfamiliar places, news of the unknown dead and wounded; some men, young and very young, were conscripted and forced to meet the war somewhere faraway, at the front or behind the front; but in the little town life went on in the time-honoured fashion, monotonously, with the minor bustle of working days, with the stagnant tranquillity of holidays, as if nothing at all were happening in the world…

'*Ja, ja! Du, herein!* In here!'

Bewildered by this tone of voice, without it even crossing his mind to ask a question or to object, Ernst went through the massive wrought iron gate of the palace. Inside the spacious entrance, a soldier in a green-grey uniform took him and showed him where he was to stand 'to attention' and then 'at ease.'

Outside the strident orders of the young officer in the black uniform could still be heard: *'Halt! Herein!'* and other people from the town now appeared, whom the solider made stand next to Ernst in a perfectly straight line.

For example, in the cool, vaulted lobby of the Palace of Culture there now appeared Yehiel Pasternak, the grocer from the corner of Slatina Street, a thin, gangly man, whose hair and beard were as yellow as straw, a man of around fifty years, whose fat wife and four children, also as blond as straw, were waiting for him at home for the Sabbath meal. The soldier in the greenish-grey uniform pointed the muzzle of his carbine at the place next to Ernst and ordered:

'Attention! At ease!'

'Yes, yes, *Herr Offitzeer*, I understand!' said Yehiel Pasternak to the soldier in a very civil voice, elevating him in rank out of fear, and stood on the precise spot indicated, as rigid as stone pillar.

'Halt! Herein!' came the officer's voice from outside. And a lad of around fifteen appeared, wearing a round black felt hat, from which poked two long curly sideburns. The lad looked around with curious blue eyes, evidently amused at what was happening to him on the holy Sabbath.

'Halt! Herein!'

And Josef Birnberg made his appearance, the owner of Forestiera L.L.C., which is to say, Limited Liability Company. Birnberg had a timber factory, forests, warehouses for firewood, lumber and railway ties, and a barrel factory. He was said to be the richest man in the town, but you could never know with those big timber merchants, because today they were as rich as a Korah and tomorrow they would suffer a resounding *krach*¹, going from boom to bust, and the whole business would come toppling down like a house of cards… A tall, imposing man with a pointy black goatee chased with strands of silver, Josef Birnberg took his place in the line, next to the *cheder*² boy with the curly sideburns and the round felt hat, answering the soldier's order in perfect German and with a perfect knowledge of German military ranks, from when he had been a sub-lieutenant in the Austro-Hungarian Army, K.u.K. Regiment, which is to say Kaiserliche und Königliche Infanterie-Regiment Nummer 77, which had earned renown in the world war of 1914-18:

'Jawohl, Gefreite! Yes, corporal!'

'Ich bin SS-Unterscharführer,' the soldier disdainfully corrected him.

Josef Birnberg looked at him in silent fear. Yes, it seemed that things had changed since then… And not only the names of the ranks, but also the tone of voice, the bearing, and who knows what else…

'Halt! Herein!' came the harsh voice from outside.

---

1 Krach - crash, literally "noise"
2 Cheder - literally, "the room, chamber," a Yiddish-language primary school, where boys up to the age of five are taught to read Hebrew and recite prayers

And Rahmil-Melamed appeared, the cheder teacher from the school for small children, who ate on weekdays at the parents' houses and on the Sabbath ate lunch at the house of Mr Josef Birnberg himself; the teacher appeared in his Sabbath kaftan, which was black, clean, patched in numerous places by his wife Sara, but so neatly worked that you could barely see where the patches were.

'*Halt!* Enter!'

And in the lobby of the Palace of Culture appeared Simon Meirovici, the poor tailor, ginger, stooped, short-sighted, who sat on the bench at the back in synagogue and rather than praying cavilled about the 'respectables' who sat by the east wall of the synagogue. After him came Zainvel, the porter in the fruit and vegetable market; then Meilach, the carter from the hay mart; then Natan Eisenguss, who owned the haberdashery and 'modes' shop in the centre of town. And so, around thirty souls of every kind had been rounded up: schoolboys, students on holiday, like Ernst, elderly men, thin and fat, fathers whose wives and children were waiting for them at home, not suspecting a thing. All these men found themselves herded into the lobby of the Palace of Culture, beneath the tall vaulted ceiling, which was painted with an ordinary blue sky, at whose edges hovered white, innocent cherubs. They were all wearing their Sabbath best, they were all Jews, all pale and frightened, and all wore the yellow star stitched to their chests and backs…

Some two weeks previously, when the order came for the Jews to stitch the yellow star to their clothes, a wave of indignation and anger washed over the community. Some said that the star should not be worn: 'We shouldn't let ourselves be humiliated.' Others said that the yellow star should be worn *'dafka'*, deliberately, with pride even: 'We should show *them* that they can't humiliate us…' But life had to go on, you had to go outside, for a loaf of bread, about your daily business, for a breath of air, and the order was categorical: 'Those who disobey will be arrested on the spot and prosecuted with the full severity of the law.' And so the second opinion prevailed and the town's Jews began to wear the yellow star, with greater or lesser pride… Moreover, the oldest and wisest of the community, with a wisdom probably springing from the ages, even found words of consolation. If a *gezeirah* had to come – an evil commandment against the Jews – then let Him Above prevent the worst, they said. In any case, many Jews, particularly the religious ones, themselves wore clothes that set them apart – caftans, round felt hats, or a kind of hat with fur in the corners, called a *streiml* – or cropped their hair short and had long curly side whiskers and untrimmed beards, to distinguish them from the other nations: 'One more distinguishing mark hardly matters, we openly declare ourselves Jews, after all, from father to son, and nobody wishes to hide…' How easily a man accustoms himself to everything! Even to his own humiliation…

To Ernst, a student who had been abroad, the law seemed not only humiliating, not only insulting, but also stupid and ridiculous. It was a small town and everybody knew everybody else, and for a fact, everybody knew who was a Jew. And who was a Romanian. And who was a Hungarian. And who was a Ukrainian. And who was a Zipser German[3]. And who was a Gypsy. Nobody tried to hide what he was. The law was quite simply idiotic. If a person knows you, what is the point of his making you wear a sign to say you are who you are? And if a person doesn't know you, what is it to him what race you are? Ernst also put these questions to his friend, Dr Klaus Daoben, the judge, who was descended from the Zipser Germans that settled in Maramureș centuries ago: a tall, muscular, suntanned man, with a round, smoothly shaven face, large head and cropped pate, a mountaineer, with whom Ernst went hiking in the Maramureș Carpathians. He put the questions to him in a bitterly joking way, but his friend did not catch the joke and answered very seriously that his duty was to judge not the laws, but only people who broke the laws,

---

3   Zipser Germans - German-speaking ethnic minority from the Zips, or Spiš, region of north-eastern Slovakia, part of the Kingdom of Hungary up to 1918

or to preside over cases filed by plaintiffs… But if the law demanded a distinguishing mark for Jews, why should it not demand a different mark for all the other races? Each with his own star or cross… Ernst even put this to Judge Daoben, as a bitter joke, for if that was how things stood, and the Jews were marked with a yellow star, then it would be only right for Hungarians to wear a green star, their favourite colour, on their chests and backs, and for Romanians to wear a blue star, and for Zipser Germans – Dr Daoben's ethnic group – to wear a black star on their chests and backs, and Ukrainians a pink star, the colour of the ribbons in their maidens' hair, and so on and so forth… And why shouldn't people also be marked according to their religion? They should wear armbands, since armbands were then very fashionable, each with a sign or symbol. Christians, a cross. Jews, the Star of David. Atheists, nothing. Which is to say, a zero… But in fact there were lots of Christian denominations and sects without a cross. The Reformed Church, for example. There were no crosses in their churches. So, let each have a letter on his armband. Catholics would have a C. Reformists an R. Baptists a B. Lutherans an L. Anabaptists an A. The Seventh-Day Adventists, who observe the Sabbath rather than Sunday, would wear an S. Jehovah's Witnesses a W, Pentecostalists a P, and so on. Every letter of the alphabet could be employed… Maybe people should also be marked according to their occupation? Barbers would have a B, for example, Merchants an M, teachers a T, doctors a D, pickpockets a PP, and so on. That way, we would know who we were dealing with at once glance. And we would treat everybody the way he deserves. Let justice be imparted equally to all… But Dr Daoben, the judge, did not laugh. He did not even smile. Probably he did not get the joke, because he replied very gravely, very seriously, that he, Judge Daoben, was required to impart justice only to those who came to court to demand it, that is, only to those who filed an official complaint, through the legal channels and with all the necessary rubber stamps…

A rigid, honest, humourless German, that judge… Yes, yes, let each bear the stigma… But in fact, it seemed that was the way things were headed. Europe was in the midst of the age of distinguishing marks, of insignia and armbands. In Germany, swastika armbands; in Italy armbands with the fasces; armbands for youths inscribed with 'Youth'; armbands for women inscribed 'Women'… Before long, there would even be a demand for armbands that simply said 'Human' – how many people would wear such an armband?

2

All of a sudden, on their way home from synagogue or after a stroll around town, the thirty men with yellow stars on their chests and backs had found themselves in the lobby of the Palace of Culture, prisoners of the SS soldiers. What did they want from them? Why had they rounded them up? Where were they going to take them? This was what they were asking themselves in their minds.

'How can I get out of this trap?' wondered Ernst, looking around him. At every door and window in the lobby was stationed a soldier in grey, holding carbines at the ready. So, there he was, a prisoner of the SS, all of a sudden, without having done anything.

The shouts of *'Halt! Herein!'* had ceased outside. The young officer in the black uniform entered the lobby and looked over that strange troop, that assembly of individuals tall and short, young and old, fat and thin, wearing elegant German suits or comical *Ost-Europeische* caftans. He paced up and down the line two or three times, visibly amused, with an ironic smile on his lips. He then came to a stop in front of the line, with his hands on his hips and his sharp elbows jutting outwards, and said in a voice unusually gentle, almost honeyed:

'*Meine Herrschaften!* Gentlemen! I have invited you here on important business for our empire, our German Reich. The quicker and the better you finish the task, the quicker you will be free. For, work alone makes man free…'

He gave a signal, two guards holding rifles stationed themselves in front of them, and the officer left.

The men in the line began to wait. What important task would they have to perform? And for the German Reich no less… And how long would it take? They asked themselves fearfully. Then, they began to calm down. In the end, the officer had not spoken rudely. On the contrary, he might even be said to have spoken politely to them. '*Meine Herrschaften*,' he had said. My gentlemen! Very *höflich*, very polite… And he had said they would be free.

They waited there, each in the same place, each standing on one of the thirty-by-thirty-centimetre, square, grey and white flagstones that covered the hall like a huge chessboard, they waited an hour, they waited two hours, three hours, the guards were changed a number of times in the meantime, men in uniform went up and down the stairs, nobody told them anything.

Ernst lost his cool:

'Why are you keeping us here pointlessly like this?' he asked one of the soldiers, addressing him in perfect German with a slight Viennese accent.

The soldier said nothing.

'What is the task we have to perform? Why doesn't anybody tell us anything?' he asked the other soldier.

He might as well have been talking to the wall.

The soldiers on guard, wearing grey-green uniforms, were changed every hour, while the men stood and waited in the same place, in a perfect line, shifting their weight from one leg to another or to both legs. The soles of their feet ached. Their bodies had become heavy, unbearably heavy. They were burning with the desire to flex their joints, to stretch out on the cold hard flagstones of the palace lobby. Their faces, which had been pale and frightened at first, had turned red with impotent fury, and then yellow, puffy from pointless waiting.

In the afternoon, at around four, they suddenly heard the rumble of large engines. Heavily laden trucks came to a stop in front of the gates of the Palace of Culture. In that instant the SS officer in the black uniform also appeared, screaming as if out of his mind:

'*Los! Los!* Move! Unload the trucks!'

There was not a trace of *meine Herrschaften* or *Höfligkeit*[4] in his screams! His reedy, strident voice was like a whip cracking over the backs of beasts of burden. The thirty, in their best clothes, exhausted from waiting, set about unloading iron bedsteads and straw mattresses from the trucks and then carried them up the stairs to the first floor. A billet for Waffen-SS soldiers in transit through the town was being readied there. A long line of heavy trucks, hundreds of iron bedsteads, and as many straw mattresses…

'Quickly! Quickly! *Schneller! Verflucht noch einmal!* Get a move on! The sooner you finish, the sooner you will be free!' yelled the officer.

And the men ran down the stairs, and then laboured back up, hauling the iron bedsteads and straw mattresses.

Up, down! Up, down! Their legs were breaking, their shoulders were aching, their clothes were tearing. They no longer felt how heavy were the iron bedsteads, they no longer felt how light and baggy were the straw mattresses, they felt only exhaustion and humiliation.

'Quickly! Quickly!'

They did not even notice when it grew dark. The lights came on. The large windows of the Palace of Culture were lit as if for a celebration, like when the town hall or a sports club or a benevolent society held a festive concert or a tea dance or a masked ball. Now, however, a strange ball indeed was being held in that fussy provincial palace, the windows were lit up festively, in stark contrast to the surrounding streets, which were plunged in darkness, and behind whose fences and dark windows waited pale folk with tearful eyes.

The news had quickly spread through the town. The streets around the building were empty. Nobody dared to set foot there. But in the nearby lanes and streets, behind the windows and fences from which it was possible to see the palace, people had gathered to wait. The parents, wives, children of those ambushed stood and waited.

---

4   Herrschaften or Hofligeit - literally the ruling classes or the nobility, meaning 'there was no trace of the great and the good'

They watched anxiously: perhaps some familiar outline might appear at a window, perhaps somebody might manage to give a sign, perhaps some news as to what was happening within might arrive.

That day, many people in town did not eat their Sabbath lunch, nor their third, *shaleshudes*[5] meal, nor the supper to bid Queen Sabbath farewell. Imperceptibly, the Sabbath, when fasting is strictly forbidden, unless it coincides with Yom Kippur, the Day of Atonement, became a long, silent, sad, fearful fast…

It was long after nightfall when the men finished furnishing the billet for the troops due to pass through the town. One by one they emerged through the wrought iron gates of the Palace of Culture, their heads bowed, their best clothes torn and dusty, humiliated and exhausted. The first to emerge was Rahmil-Melamed, the teacher to small children, his Sabbath caftan, so beautifully patched by the hand of his wife Sara, now in tatters. All the people from the dark side streets rushed up to him, asking what had been going on and what had happened to the others. Then Yehiel Pasternak appeared, the grocer whose hair and beard were as yellow as straw, and he was bent in two at the hips. Then came Mr Iosef Birnberg, the proprietor of Forestiera Ltd., his clothes and dignity as a former officer of a Kaiserliche und Königliche Infantry Regiment now completely rumpled. Next to slip through the palace gates were Zainvel, who worked as a porter in the fruit and vegetable market, and the *cheder* boy with his curly side whiskers, sucking his bleeding finger, and Natan Eisenguss, who owned a shop for ladies' *modes*, and Simon Meirovici, the poor tailor and patcher. They slipped through the gates without a word of complaint, they hurried away, without looking back, heading for their homes, along with those who had been waiting for them outside, all of them breathing sighs of relief and thanking the Lord Above that they had got off so lightly.

At the time, they thought they had got off lightly…

---

5   Shaleshudes - the "third meal" eaten to mark the Sabbath, after the afternoon prayer

3

But only twenty-nine of the thirty Jews emerged from the gates of the palace, heads bowed, humiliated and exhausted, and went home. One alone, Ernst, remained inside much longer. His father, mother, elder brothers and sisters-in-law waited despairingly on a dark side street, from where the wrought iron gate of the Palace of Culture and festively lit windows were visible. That light, which in days gone by used to be accompanied by orchestra music, the sounds of balls, parties, merriment, clinking glasses, the rhythms of the dance, now seemed cold and ironic. It poured from the building to the accompaniment of opaque silence and spread over the street in long swaths. Why didn't Ernst come out already? Why didn't they let him go? Might he have defied them? He was so disobedient. And irascible. And reckless. Being the youngest son, he had always been the most spoiled. Might he have believed that he could do what he liked there too? Or that he could refuse to do what he was ordered? What could they be doing to him in there, now that he was alone with them? His old father, with his white hair and side whiskers *à la Franz Josef*, trembling with annoyance, and next to him his tall mother, as thin as a plank, and behind them the two elder brothers and two docile daughters-in-law, stood in the dark alley, gazing fixedly at the illuminated building. It was as if they had turned to stone. They felt neither weariness nor the passing time.

Ernst's parents' concern was not unfounded. After the men had finished arranging the iron bedsteads and straw mattresses, and twenty-nine of them had been released, the SS officer, who from the very start had singled him out, perhaps because of his clenched jaw and the scowl of his green eyes as he worked, asked Ernst, without any reason, but from a certain intuition: 'What is your name?'

The young officer, with his immaculate black uniform, had not asked anybody else that question, and his interest did not bode well.

'Ernst... Ernst Blumenthal is my name.'

It was plain that the officer was unpleasantly surprised.

'Ernst? Ernst?' he muttered. Such first names when applied to 'that lot' quite simply infuriated him. Abraham, Isaak, Yakov, yes! Chaim, Shmil, even better! Israel, highly appropriate! But Ernst? Completely out of line! Barefaced cheek! And what was more, his surname was Blumenthal... Which is to say, 'Flower Vale.' Beautiful German surnames like that being used by *Ost-Juden*, by those non-Aryan Orientals, offended his aesthetic sense, nothing less. It was the same as calling a mangy, bearded billy-goat a thoroughbred stallion... The blood rose to his head, but he controlled himself and asked, almost politely:

'What is your occupation?'

'I'm a student.'

Quite simply exasperating. An Ernst. And a Blumenthal. And a student to boot.

'What are you studying?'

'Architecture.'

The officer in the black uniform was seething. His small green eyes were giving off sparks. His chiselled features looked even sharper.

'Where are you a student?'

'In Vienna. I have broken off my studies temporarily, because of the... the situation.'

He had been about to say 'because of the Anschluss between Austria and the German Reich,' but stopped himself in time.

The officer's face turned red. This was the very limit! An Ernst, and a Blumenthal, and an architectural student, in Vienna no less. He felt like shooting him on the spot with his revolver. But he controlled himself and after a few moments said in an ironically urbane voice:

'It means we are colleagues. I am a student too, of art history, in Berlin. I too have broken off my studies, temporarily, because of the situation… And since you, colleague, are so terribly knowledgeable about architecture, I shall give you the opportunity to do something for this secession style palace, *à la Franz Josef*, which Zarathustra alone knows why the Austro-Hungarian Emperor had built in this stinking little town! You will clean all the dirt and straw you have left on these stairs.'

The lobby of the palace was magnificent. Broad white steps of marbled stone led to the two upper floors. The steps were edged with strips of bronze. It was true: the steps were strewn with bits of straw that had fallen out of the mattresses.

'What are you looking for, colleague?' the officer asked, sarcastically.

'A broom.'

'Oh, no! That would be blasphemy! This is a delicate task. It must be done by hand.'

Ernst gazed at him for a long moment. He could not believe his ears. What? Why was he suggesting such a thing? To collect that straw, bit by bit, with his bare hands. The means had no connection with the end… Cleanliness and order… The only object was to humiliate him. He stood where he was for a few moments. The officer made a gesture with his hand. Ernst looked in amazement at that delicate white hand, with its long fingers, like a pianist's, which quivered tensely next to the handle of the revolver. He stooped and clenching his jaws, he began to collect the straw from the steps.

The officer left. He returned about an hour later.

'I have finished,' Ernst said. 'Can I go now?'

'You have not finished!' replied the officer with restrained fury, scrutinising the steps. He pointed to an inch-long bit of straw wedged in a crack between two steps.

Ernst picked up the bit of straw and set about examining the steps from top to bottom. The officer went away again. He returned about two hours later.

'I've finished!' said Ernst.

'I will tell you *when* you have finished and *if* you have finished, colleague!' All of a sudden he switched to a disdainful plural: 'You lot should learn once and for all how to work properly! And you should stop being liars, the lot of you!'

The officer inspected the steps of the palace once again, all the way up to the second floor, and pointed to an almost invisible bit of straw, lodged in an indentation of the wrought iron bannister.

The officer left. Ernst went on searching. He felt as if his shame and impotent rage would suffocate him. Maybe he would keep him there all night. Maybe he would keep him there for days, weeks. He would always be able to find a bit of straw hidden somewhere. And even without finding any more straw, he could keep him there as long as he liked. He was completely in his hands. In those delicate white hands, with their long fingers, like a pianist's, the hands of that student of art history from Berlin…

It was almost midnight when the young officer in the black uniform came back, his face puffy, his eyes glistening with drink. Ernst sensed his presence, but did not look at him and did not say a word.

'Well, now you can leave!' shouted the officer, sarcastically. 'But don't think you have finished, colleague! We shall meet again…'

Ernst did not understand those words. What did he mean? Why would they meet again? Was it an idle threat, or did he know something?

But not even the officer realised how prophetic his words would turn out to be. He did not know that they would indeed meet again, but in a completely different situation, in circumstances so strange, so absurd, that no sane mind could ever have imagined them…

4

It was almost midnight when Ernst Blumenthal emerged through the wrought iron gates of the Palace of Culture, in the secession style *à la Franz Josef*. As soon as his elderly father, with his grizzled side whiskers, also *à la Franz Josef*, espied him, trembling with emotion, he breathed a sigh of relief, as did his mother, tall and thin as a plank, his two elder brothers, and the two docile daughters-in-law. Praise be to God! Praise be to Him, that he had got off so lightly!

But Ernst did not breathe a sigh of relief for having got off so lightly. In the first place because 'so lightly' was not very lightly at all, and in the second place because he did not believe he had 'got off'… In the days and nights that followed, he had no peace of mind. He kept thinking about what had happened, he went over it all in his mind, striving to find a meaning to it.

How then had things unfolded? A young foreign officer, a stranger from another land, from another world, had arrived in the centre of town and in broad daylight sequestered thirty citizens of that town, who had been walking down the street minding their own business, and no authority had taken action, there was no authority with which one might lodge a complaint… And what if one did make a complaint? And what if the authority did decide to take action? What action might it take? What it meant was that the collection of bits of straw with one's bare hands was not over… It meant that although he had been set free at midnight, he was not free. All of them were prisoners: Ernst, the town's citizens, the authorities, the enforcers of the law, the law itself… But people did not realise it. They walked down the street, they breathed, they went about their business, as if nothing were happening. Those who had been sequestered rejoiced at having been released, others rejoiced at the fact that nothing had happened to them. They were all rejoicing.

Ernst felt like laughing out loud.

Rumours began to circulate around town. Young men were being called up to serve in the army. Even those who had already done their national service received orders to enlist. The Jews who were enlisted were not given rifles. They were untrustworthy. Nor were they given uniforms, because they were unworthy of the *Magyar Királyi Honvéd*, which is to say the Royal Hungarian Army, the army of a kingdom without a king, where reigned a kind of Admiral Regent, without a fleet and without a sea, an admiral who liked always to be photographed riding a white horse. An equestrian navy.

They were not worthy to wear a uniform or to bear arms. On the other hand, the Jews who were enlisted received yellow armbands, to be worn on their left arms, and a pick or a shovel. That did not bode well. Armbands, and yellow to boot. The Jews had new impressions and old memories, very old memories, to do with the colour yellow… It was rumoured that the young men, wearing their own clothes from home, but now with yellow armbands, and carrying picks or shovels over their shoulders, were to serve in labour brigades.

Not long after the rumours, those slips of paper did indeed begin to arrive, call-up papers, printed SAS in bold letters. Who knows what those letters meant? Maybe 'Eagle,' maybe 'Lightning.' They meant you had to pack your suitcase and quickly enlist. You didn't have time to think about it. And those slips of paper were followed by yet more rumours, that the labour battalions were being sent over the border, to the front. They said that some of them had gone all the way to the Don Bend. And there they dug trenches, built shelters, lugged shells to the front line. Some were sent to clear minefields with their bare hands. Clearing them was only a manner of speaking. In fact, those soldiers without weapons and without uniforms, dressed in their civilian clothes, with yellow armbands, were forced to run across the minefields so that the mines would explode under them … But people said a lot of things. How could you know where the truth ended and the lies began?

Ernst did not want to wait to be called up. Why should he wait? And what awaited him? That officer in the immaculate black uniform had predicted that they would meet again. Ernst had no desire whatever to lay eyes on him again. That day of toil, or rather humiliation, under his command, had been an excellent lesson. They were under occupation. The town had become a prison with invisible walls, and he had to escape from those walls. He had to leave for a time, to disappear into the mountains. He knew the mountain paths; he knew many hiding places. He had hiked the length and breadth of those mountains. He knew houses where hospitable mountain folk lived; he knew sheepfolds where the shepherds made cheese and told stories around the fire at night.

One evening, after a meal eaten in tense silence, Ernst told his parents that he intended to go up into the mountains for a while, to take a long excursion. His mother began to weep softly. What else could she do? Mrs Bertha Blumenthal was a tall, thin woman, a frightened woman. When she had cause for joy, she wept, because she was frightened of the evil eye, and when she suffered a misfortune, she wept for fear that she had fallen victim to the evil eye. Ernst's elder brothers, Nathan and Matthias, tried to persuade him to stay at home, and the two docile daughters-in-law nodded. 'Stay at home,' the brothers advised, 'don't part from the family.' Which was absurd, to say the least, because if the order came for him to enlist, he would have to part from the family anyway. Only his father said nothing. Ever since the day when Ernst had been sequestered in the Palace of Culture, his father had been worried. He knew his youngest son. He was not like his elder brothers. They were settled, disciplined, prudent. If some authority, it didn't matter which authority, or somebody in uniform, it didn't matter which uniform, had ordered them to pick up bits of straw from a flight of stairs, they would have done so without a murmur, they had a well-honed instinct for survival, they would have striven not to draw attention to themselves. But Ernst was irascible by nature, unruly, he was quick to lose his temper. It was a miracle that that officer had not hit him over the head with one of those iron bedsteads, God forbid! That would have been all they needed!

His mother wept, his brothers talked, his sisters-in-law nodded docilely, his father was silent. Ernst's mind was made up.

Ernst was a taciturn young man. He spoke sparingly and did not feel the need to justify his decisions. He was a stubborn young man, with a prominent, clenched jaw, middling in height, sturdy. His bronzed face was angular, as if whittled from hard oak. He wore his hair cropped short and combed back, so that it bristled like a coarse brush. He was a sportsman, a mountaineer. He knew all the Carpathian hills and mountains that surrounded the town. He knew the peaks and the valleys, the crags and the caves, each by its name. He knew the paths and the trails. He loved the mountains and was convinced that the time had come for them to repay his love by protecting him.

His mother lamented: Who would take care of him there, alone in the forest? Who would cook for him? Who would wash his clothes? Who would darn his socks? Ernst's brothers tried to calm her; his father was silent. Ernst laughed softly at his mother's ridiculous questions and tried to soothe her. A man isn't alone up there in the mountains. In any event, he's no more alone than in the middle of the most crowded city… True, there are no taps with hot or cold water, but there are springs and brooks of pure, clear water. And there are houses with shingled and thatched roofs in which to shelter, dotted over the hills and along the valleys. He knew those wooden houses well. In Vienna he had written a dissertation on the architecture of the peasant houses of Maramureş, which had drawn the favourable attention of his professors.

Up in the mountains there were sheepfolds with taciturn shepherds, sheep peacefully grazing, small, sturdy, thick-furred sheepdogs guarding against the wolves. Over the summer he would be able to survive very well, under a roof of leaves, with maize porridge and milk and whey and cold spring water. He would find shelter by a sheepfold or in the house of welcoming folk. Perhaps, Ernst thought to himself, he would seek shelter in the house of Simion Vlașin, on Agrișul Hill, who kept a milk cow, hens and geese, and who in winter chopped cartloads of firewood to sell in the town below. Often, when he went on excursions, Ernst would stop off in Simion Vlașin's yard to rest from the tiring climb, on the porch, where he would drink a cup of frothing milk fresh from the cow. In the vast space of the mountains, where people were so sparse and lived so far from one another, they felt closer to one another than people in the town, who lived cramped together in their housing blocks. There, hospitality was a powerful, unwritten rule: if you are a stranger, the mountain man does not ask you who you are, where you are from, where you are going, when you turn up at his gate, but invites you into his house, to his table, and regales you with whatever he has: an unleavened loaf, a cup of milk, a chunk of sheep's cheese. But no, he would not go to stay with Simion Vlașin, who had a hard life, with six children and a seventh on the way. Naturally, wherever he stayed, he would pay for his lodging, but at Vlașin's house there was little room and many children's mouths, which, unwittingly, might let slip an unguarded word and give away his hiding place.

Somewhat higher up the hill, about three kilometres from Simion Vlașin's homestead, was the house of Ionu Stan, known as 'Son of the Trustworthy One,' after his late father, who was an industrious and wise peasant, also called Ionu Stan, but whom folk had nicknamed 'The Trustworthy One,' because all his life he had been a man in whom trust was placed, in other words, he was a forest warden. A small man, with an unruly beard and a face covered with scratches and scars, made by branches and thorns, with fierce, glowering eyes, he roamed the forest with an old flintlock, longer than him, scaring off poachers, but turning a blind eye when some poor man cut himself a cartload of deadwood to burn in his stove or hunted a rabbit without a licence from the Compossessoratus. His son, Ionu Stan, Son of the Trustworthy One, had, astonishingly, inherited not only the exact same appearance, but also the position, flintlock, gentle nature and wisdom of his father.

Yes, thought Ernst, he would take shelter in his homestead for a few weeks, for a month or two, until the storm passed. It couldn't last long. After Stalingrad, the Germans were constantly 'falling back to previously prepared positions, causing the Russian hordes heavy losses,' as the newspapers put it. And in the spring of that year, 1944, the 'hordes' had reached the eastern flanks of the Maramureş Carpathians, beyond Iaşina, which is to say, the border of the sub-Carpathian region of the then Hungary, where they had halted, turning their offensive southward, in the direction of Jassy. And the Red Army waited there, over the Carpathians, for many months, until Maramureş, which at the time belonged to Hungary, became *Judenfrei*, cleansed of Jews…

But Ernst Blumenthal did not know what was to happen in the spring of 1944, he knew only that he should not wait to be enlisted in a forced labour battalion or to have another encounter with young officers who studied art history in Berlin, but rather he should hide, vanish into the mountains he loved and whose turn had come to grant him protection.

Ernst was not superstitious, but it seemed to him that he saw it as a sign from Above, or from Destiny, whatever you choose to call it, when Ionu Son of the Trustworthy One came to his house that very same Friday morning. Friday was the day when Ionu came to market to sell his eggs and sheep's cheese. Beforehand he paid visits to people he knew, selling them his wares, and then he went to the market to sell what was left over and to buy salt and gas, as they called lamp oil in Maramureş. Ernst took him aside and told him that he was going to come to Agriş, on a lengthier excursion than usual. Ionu blinked his small eyes, which were as dark as peppercorns. He understood very well what Ernst meant. Ernst gave him some money and asked him to buy him some peasant clothes, which should not be too worn: a pair of frieze trousers, a thick homespun shirt, a jerkin, a straw hat with an ostrich feather, of the kind young men wore in the Iza Valley, and a knapsack, of the kind worn slung over one shoulder, with a pouch in front and one behind. And not to say anything to anybody.

The peasant blinked his small, dark peppercorn eyes and by that evening Ernst had a pouch containing the items in his room.

In the Blumenthal household, that Saturday was sad and oppressive. Ernst's mother sighed, his brothers paced restlessly from room to room, and his old father, with his rosy face framed by grizzled hair and bushy side whiskers *à la Franz Josef*, stubbornly kept his eyes fastened on a book, without seeing the letters, but only the black of their rows. And all were silent. There was nothing more to be said. On Sunday morning, at the crack of dawn, through the door of the Blumenthal house a peasant slipped outside into the street, a short, sturdy young man, with a bronzed, angular face, as if whittled from oak, and with a jutting jawbone. He was dressed in a coat and trousers of thick frieze and had a knapsack slung over his left shoulder. He turned down the lane that led to Mill Park, which lay at the bottom of Solovan Hill.

The streets were deserted. Silence. The air was fresh and cool. Ernst took a deep breath. He had got off to a good start, a very good start, even. There was nobody out and about at that hour to see him, and even if somebody had seen him, that person would not have seen Ernst Blumenthal, erstwhile student of architecture in Vienna, candidate for a forced labour battalion and mine clearing at the front, but rather a Maramureș peasant, wearing peasant shoes and a straw hat with an ostrich feather, who was on his way to Solovan Hill.

All of a sudden, he felt like laughing. Good God, how many ridiculous mistakes could a man make! First of all, he oughtn't to have set off on a Sunday of all days. What peasant travels from the town to the village on a Sunday? On Sunday, the peasants of Maramureș, wearing their best clothes, stay in the village, they sit on the benches in front of their houses, or in the road in front of the mayor's office or the church, and they chat about what is happening in the village and in the town, in the land and in the world. And what peasant carries a heavy knapsack on his back on a Sunday? In the end, if anybody had been curious enough to see what was in that double knapsack, he would have been astounded and prompted to make the sign of the cross: what kind of peasant went around with a toothbrush and tubes of toothpaste in his knapsack? Not to mention novels, the fifth volume of an architectural treatise, sketchbooks and coloured pencils. And a large pair of binoculars… A peasant with binoculars!

But the streets were deserted, all was quiet, and the air was fresh and cool. There was no other soul to be seen, no sound to be heard, not even the sound of Ernst's footsteps, since he trod on the pillows of leather soles. He walked down a number of side streets, then down the street that led to Morii Park, flanked by lindens and horse chestnuts, and came to the River Iza, which flowed yellow and sluggish at the bottom of Solovan Hill. He climbed the narrow wooden bridge, a cart's width wide, with the thought of crossing quickly and then vanishing among the paths that wound between the briars and trees, leading up the hill. But reaching the middle of the wooden bridge, he suddenly came to a stop, taking fright. At the other end of the bridge, by the spring of clear water that poured through a small wooden trough at the bottom of Solovan Hill, and which was called Pintea's Spring, Ernst espied a military tent of dirty khaki. The barrel of a gun poked through the flap of the tent. Ernst stood stock still, as if rooted to the spot. The round steel eye of the gun barrel gazed at him motionlessly. Ernst stood still, as if hypnotised by the gaze. Alone there on the wooden bridge, he was obviously the perfect target in the sights of the carbine. Just one detonation, and his entire journey, barely begun, would be over. There, at the gateway to the town…

Ernst looked into the barrel of the gun. The gun looked back at him, motionless. Yes, it was not moving. Ernst came to his senses. His mind began to work feverishly. It meant that neither was the man behind the gun moving. He plucked up courage, gripped the haft of the hunting knife inside his pocket, and slowly, softly resumed crossing the bridge. In his leather moccasins he trod as if on cotton wool. He made no sound. He moved closer and closer toward the barrel of the carbine. He reached the tent and cast a glance through the flaps. Within, the soldier on guard was lying on the ground, fast asleep, his head resting on the rifle butt. He was a reservist, quite old, in a rumpled and patched *honvéd* uniform, albeit buttoned up to the neck in regulation fashion. The pointed military cap, with a rosette, was pulled down tightly over the sweating head, and from beneath it, at the temples, poked bristles of grey hair. The face was bony, heavy jawed, deeply furrowed, sunburnt. The face of a peasant from the Panonian steppe.

The man suddenly moved his head and began to breathe like a bellows. Ernst quickly went around the tent and climbed the hill. After reaching the top, by winding paths and shortcuts, he stopped to catch his breath.

From there, in the clear morning air, he could see the town below, with its red roofs of tile or sheet metal coated with red lead, and its white roofs of galvanised zinc. Amid the roofs soared the spires of the churches, the fortress-like turrets of the Palace of Culture, and the bastions of the so-called Redoubt, where the town's cinema was housed and on whose upper floor the Military Club held balls, and where on Sundays and national holidays the military band played rousing marches. From the top of Solovan Hill could also be seen the town's two-storey buildings (there were no three-storey buildings): the boys' lyceum, the teachers' college, the intricate tracery of the façade of the girl's gymnasium school, and the old, drab prefecture and town hall. Also visible were the four large synagogues, but the dozens of houses of prayer, scattered all over town, alongside the ordinary houses, could not be made out. Spreading from the edge of town could be seen the Bulgarians' gardens, with their perfectly rectangular vegetable patches, in every shade of green, and the peasants' maize fields, flanked by rows of sunflowers, and the swift Tisza and the yellow, sluggish Iza, which enclosed the town, making it an island. Below him, at the bottom of Solovan Hill he could see the dirty green of the khaki canvas tent, in which the soldier was fast asleep, his head resting on the stock of his rifle. That poor soldier was sleeping peacefully, without any inkling of the danger he had been in. If he had stopped him and asked for his papers, Ernst would have jumped on him and stabbed him in the belly with his knife. What else could he have done?

But would he really have done it? And if he had tried to make a run for it, would the soldier really have shot him? He would have shot him without a doubt. He had his orders, after all.

But what was that dirty green khaki canvas tent doing there anyway? What was that peasant from somewhere in the distant Hortobágy, from the Hungarian steppe, doing there in that mountain landscape, pointing a gun at the town? They had obviously posted sentinels at all the exits from the town. So quickly have the prison walls closed in on us, thought Ernst. But only on us? The war had reached the border. Wasn't the soldier's rifle pointed threateningly at all the town's citizens? Wouldn't anybody at all be ordered to halt?

Just yesterday, the prison was a big as the whole country. You couldn't enter or leave unsupervised. Now, the town was a prison, surrounded by invisible walls and guarded by soldiers. And tomorrow? What would tomorrow bring? The streets and then the houses would become prisons. And the walls would close in more and more narrowly, and every person would be a prison unto himself. And a prison guard unto himself…

That evening Ernst arrived at the house of Ionu, Son of the Trustworthy One, over Argriş Hill. He had travelled by hidden paths, he had climbed the hills by steep shortcuts, untrodden by Sunday excursionists, whom you saw strolling along the winding paths, pausing from time to time to admire the landscape from the foot of Solovan Hill or sitting in a circle on the grass in the glades, peacefully eating sandwiches, drinking steaming coffee from thermos flasks, and avidly inhaling the pure air, as if performing a ritual. A sacred ritual: the inhalation of pure mountain air.

Ernst emerged from the fir trees and on the smooth, gentle slope of the hill saw the house of Ionu Stan, known as Son of the Trustworthy One. The house was made of oak beams and had a tapering shingle roof, blackened by age and wood smoke. The house did not have a chimney, and in winter, the smoke from the stove rose into the attic and seeped out through the shingles. The whole roof used to smoke, like a huge tobacco pipe, laid on a snow-white tablecloth.

But it was not winter now and no smoke seeped through the roof. In the dusk all the surroundings were deep green, apart from the house, blackened by time and soot, and the narrow path that led to it, which was clayey yellow in the fading light.

Suddenly, a large sheepdog, with a round, stocky body covered in thick white fur, rushed furiously from the yard towards the approaching stranger. Ernst did not take fright. He sat down on the ground and there he remained, motionless. The dog circled him a few times and then stopped in front of him, growling contentedly. Ernst knew the dog. And the dog knew him. A few years previously, when he had approached the house for the first time, the dog had rushed out furiously, like a white cannonball. That time he had taken fright. He had been about to run away or to defend himself with his mountaineer's cane. But Ionu Son of the Trustworthy One had shouted to him from the porch, telling him to sit down on the grass where he was and not to move. Ernst had sat down on the ground and waited, stock-still. The dog had circled him a few times, looking at him with its small red eyes. Ernst had then slowly stood up and the dog had escorted him at a distance of a few paces into its master's yard.

5

Back then things always took the same course when he stopped off at Agriș Hill on a day trip. He would sit down with his fellow wayfarers on the bench on the veranda to drink a jug of fresh milk, to sample a slice of new cheese, and to chat with Ionu, who, although he lived up in the mountains, without a radio, without newspapers, was surprisingly well informed about what went on in the rest of the country and in foreign parts.

Back then it was pleasant, the days were serene, and he used to be greeted with: 'Welcome, young sir!' and on leaving they would bid him: 'Farewell, young sir!' It was tranquil and pleasing aromas wafted on the pure air.

But now it was completely different. He had arrived in the house of Ionu Stan, Son of the Trustworthy One, as a kind of clandestine tenant, on an unlimited stay, paying for his board and lodgings. Disguised to look like one of them, although he was not one of them, but rather a young sir from town, dressed in peasant's frieze trousers and hemp smock, with rustic moccasins and a straw hat adorned with an ostrich feather, garb he wore quite awkwardly.

They all felt embarrassed. Ernst tried to strike up a conversation with Ionu:

'It was hot today.'

'Hot.'

'But the weather is getting cooler.'

'It's getting cooler.'

The host's three children, the eldest daughter, Eudochia, who was old enough to marry, and the two younger ones, Andilina, who was fourteen, and Ionuț, the little lad of six, gazed at the familiar stranger, who had visited their house many times but who now had come dressed in peasant garb. He would have to give them an explanation… In the meantime, it had grown dark and Ileana, the forester's wife, a strong woman a head taller than her husband, had lit the oil lamp. The flames sputtered, casting shadows over the whitewashed walls of the house, they roared high, like monsters, and then docilely quieted down, while the wick desperately sucked in air. The lamp began to crackle, the flame settled, casting a yellow light on their faces.

Ileana had completed four years of schooling there in the mountains, at the primary school in the hamlet of Sihei, at the foot of Agriș Hill, after which she had lived for a few years in the town, in the house of Father Ion Bîrcea. The priest's wife, Adriana, in order to help her husband and increase his rather modest income, had set up a carpet-weaving workshop in their yard. Ileana and other girls from the country worked on traditional Maramureș carpets in the workshop. A clever, playful woman, with a certain amount of town education and with the wisdom instilled in her at home, Ileana was the first to find the right tone to dissipate the awkwardness:

'In these parts, young sir, we call to each other from the neighbouring hilltops by name, like this: Gheo–, Pa–, Ste– . How should we call you? Er–?'

They all laughed and the ice melted.

'You oughtn't to call me at all!' said Ernst gravely. 'You know very well that I'm here, but in fact I'm not here…'

Ileana took the cauldron from the large stove, which occupied around a quarter of the room.

'Take a seat at the table, young sir.'

The cauldron of maize porridge crackled and smoked. They all sat down around the table. None of the dishes from the great Sacher Restaurant in central Vienna was as tasty as that maize porridge and whey.

No doubt about it: clothes don't make the man, but rather they conceal him. He was still a young sir from the town. True, his face was sunburned, but his hands were those of a town dweller, with slender, nervous fingers. All of a sudden, Ileana, the forester's wife, burst out laughing. She looked intently at the hands of their new lodger. It was only now that Ernst noticed that he had forgotten to take off his gold signet ring, embossed with his monogram. A peasant with a gold signet ring? Such a thing was unheard of in the mountains of Maramureş, even if you walked their length and breadth…

They all made merry around the table.

After supper, Ileana urged her husband – Ionu was a man slow to react – to make up a bed for the 'young sir.' Which is to say, to make up the only bed in the house: the others slept in the main room – Ionu, Ileana and their eldest daughter Eudochia on the chests that lined the three walls, and the two youngest, Andilina and Ion, on the shelf behind the stove.

Ionu had bought the only bed in the house a long while ago, without planning to do so beforehand, at the big fair in Sighet: he had liked the light pinewood, stained light brown, and above all he had liked the two white doves carved on the tall headboard, on whose beaks rested a large red heart. Sweating and triumphant, Ionu had carted the bed back from the fair. The whole family had liked it, but when night fell, nobody had wanted to sleep in it. Ileana and Ionu himself, along with their daughter Eudochia, preferred the chests in the main room, and neither of the two youngest children had wanted to abandon the large, warm stove behind which they slept. And so the beautiful bed with the red heart and white doves had remained unused, in the narrow chamber next to the main room.

The hosts were overjoyed to have the opportunity to provide the young sir from town with town-like accommodation.

But nor did Ernst feel at ease in the large bed in the small chamber. Perhaps because the straw mattress was too hard, packed too tightly, or perhaps because of the feather duvet, which was stuffed not only with down, but with whole feathers, which pricked him through the cloth. Or perhaps because with the coming of night a shadow of fear also descended, thickening the darkness.

Nor did the host, Ionu Stan Son of the Trustworthy One sleep peacefully that night. Ernst could hear him tossing and turning and then going out onto the veranda to breathe some fresh air. Or perhaps he went out merely to gaze at the stars? Or perhaps a fine coating of fear had settled on his soul too?

Towards morning, Ernst, exhausted, drifted off and finally fell into a deep, dreamless sleep. He was awoken by the rays of the already risen sun, which poured down warmly over the cool uplands.

Although his hosts had left a basin and a mug of water for him on a stool in the corner of the room, Ernst did not wash inside the house. He took his towel and a fragment of soap and went down to the stream in the valley. The water was cold, invigorating. Ernst rinsed with a little water and then rubbed his chest and back with the towel. His skin reddened and he felt well. He went into the house to eat breakfast. A flat loaf of maize bread, fresh from the oven, was waiting for him, and cottage cheese and a mug of milk. The family had long since eaten and gone off to do their chores. The children had gone down to the school in Sihei. Ionu, before going to guard the woods, was busy in the barn, where he kept a cow, after which he would muck out the hencoops.

Ernst went into the barn and called Ionu into the house, because he wished to speak to him and Ileana.

They sat down at the table and Ernst told them that there was no point, nor was it proper, that he stay in the house. Relatives and friends of the family would come to visit and ask all kinds of questions. People are curious by nature: 'Who's that man? Where's he from?' 'A relative.' 'What kind of relative? How come I've never seen him before?'… No, he would spend the day outside, in the forest, and he would come to the house to eat when he was hungry. He would come inside only when he was sure there were no visitors there. And in the evening, he would cross the fence by the stile at the back of the house and sleep in the hayloft of the barn. The children shouldn't tell anybody he was staying there. They were old enough to understand.

His hosts remained silent. It was obvious they were in a quandary.

'I like to sleep in haylofts. That's what I do when I'm hiking,' said Ernst.

Ionu Stan remained silent for a long time. He was somewhat embarrassed, but ultimately satisfied with the proposal. After a time, he said:

'If you think it will be better that way –'

And Ileana added: 'Yes, yes, if that's the way the gentleman wants it.'

Ernst went outside and found himself in the vastness of the Agriş Valley, surrounded by forests. He was free. For the first time in his life, Ernst was free in the truest sense of the word. He had nothing to do, no business to attend to. He did not feel any need to read a book. He did not wish to look through the newspapers or to arrange a date with a girl. He did not have to be home at set times to eat meals with his family. He did not have to work on the designs for some house or villa, to fray his nerves because of some irascible, snobbish patron or because of some rival young architect cleverer than him. This was what had happened three months previously, when he had designed a villa, but the patron had opted for the plans drawn up by another architect, because he had put a completely pointless and unsightly turret above the front door. But it was precisely that turret that had delighted the patron, who had accepted the design, compensating Ernst with a niggardly sum for the hours of work he had invested.

No, there was nothing to fray Ernst's nerves up here. He was free and he felt like gambolling through that vast space, gambolling, running like a thoroughbred dog released from its master's leash. He felt like rolling down that immense valley, which was as round as a cauldron, rolling down to the bottom, where stood a solitary, lightning-blasted tree, and then, thanks to the momentum he would gain, rolling up the other side and back down again.

He had an unquenchable thirst to walk. He reached the lightning-blasted tree. It was a large, magnificent oak, which had been struck many years ago. Since then, it had stood majestic, powerful, its thick roots and black leafless branches infinitely confronting Time. The tree had not rotted. It had a large hollow, the inside of which was scorched. The soot had in time hardened and gleamed like ebony.

All around that broad valley, over the hills that rose from its rim, there were groves of oak trees at the edges of the forests of tall firs. Higher up, the vegetation thinned, and stunted pines dotted the mountaintops.

The whole of that realm of silence now belonged to Ernst Blumenthal. But like every realm of that kind, it also had an egress to the land of people and cares… At the top of Solovan Hill there was an old wooden watchtower, which had once served as a lookout post for spotting fires. From the tower it was possible to see the town of Sighet in the valley, clasped between two rivers: the Tisza and the Iza.

Ernst looked down at the town. Viewed from up there, it looked as small as a toy, and the people were small too, as they went about their petty business.

The town's age-old tranquillity was not to last for long. The time was mid-April, in the year 1944. Ernst lay in the grass, among the trees, his hiding place by the lookout post on Solovan Hill, and gazed at an anthill. Each ant was working assiduously, carrying heavy weights: seeds, all kinds of crumbs. They moved rapidly back and forth, without bumping into each other, without traffic accidents, without workplace accidents. It was something admirable and wholly incomprehensible.

All of a sudden, as if in a dream, he seemed to hear strange sounds from the town in the valley below: weeping and wailing, sighs, yes, even the sighs reached up into the mountains, wafting ever higher. Ernst quickly climbed the watchtower and looked through his binoculars at that other anthill. A human anthill. Along the town's streets, motley columns of people, carrying heavy suitcases, pillows, quilts, some of them pushing handcarts, were all heading in the same direction, towards the western edge of the town, where there were a brickworks and the poorest residential quarter.

What did it mean? What was happening down there? Ernst wondered in alarm. He would ask Ionu Stan to go into town straightaway and find out what was happening.

Ionu took his knapsack with the two canisters – the house had almost run out of lamp oil and matches – and went into town. He returned that evening and the news he brought was not at all encouraging. The Blumenthals' house was shut up, the door sealed by the town hall. And all the Jews had been taken to the tanners' quarter and the brickworks. It was not possible to enter the quarter because a barbed wired fence had been erected and gendarmes with cockerel feathers in their caps guarded the entrances.

Ernst chanced to discover more a few days later. He was coming down Meia Hill when he spotted a group of excursionists climbing his way. He knew where they would stop for a picnic and so he concealed himself in some undergrowth. The excursionists came closer and Ernst was amazed to see his old acquaintances, the group in whose company he had used to go on outings.

Dr Daoben, the tall, bony, suntanned judge, was climbing the hill, alongside his wife, a strong, muscular, taciturn woman, who always let her husband put forth his opinions without interrupting him. Behind them, puffing and panting, came lawyer and notary public Zeleznay. Short, plump, he leaned on a hunting cane, which, when thrust in the earth, also served as a seat. He was accompanied by his wife, a garrulous, anxious woman, who was always worried about her husband's health, fearful lest he be struck by a bout of apoplexy. At every step she begged him to stop and take a breather. They lived next door to the Blumenthals; a plank fence separated their back yards. The two couples were attended by Pritko, who obligingly ran back and forth between them.

This Pritko – nobody knew his first name, and if Pritko was his first name, then nobody knew his surname – was a kind of town idiot, who accompanied excursionists of every walk in life, from the highest to the lowest. He was a bachelor, always rather unwashed, rather longhaired, rather unshaven. He used to talk about big subjects, such as the creation of the world, whether God existed, what would happen at the end of the world. It was said that he had once studied chemistry at university, but because of an unrequited love, he had ended up in the Sighet Mental Hospital, which after a time had discharged him with the assessment 'placid, not a danger to society.' At home, rather than a cat or a dog, he kept two snakes: a large python in a chest with lots of air holes, and a smaller, non-venomous snake from the Solovan Mountains.

Ernst hid among the trees at the edge of the clearing where the excursionists sat down on the soft grass. Mrs Zeleznay, the notary public's wife, laid a white tablecloth on the grass, on which the picnickers placed loaves of bread, cheeses, pastrami and the other good things they had brought from home. Pritko lit a fire, over which he placed a griddle for the trout he had skilfully caught with his bare hands in the clear stream in the valley they had crossed.

Judge Rudolf Daoben continued the conversation he had begun:

'Whatever you might say, colleague Zeleznay, there has never been such an avalanche of laws. They're not allowed to hold public office, to work as functionaries in town or village halls. Not even the most rundown village in the back of beyond is allowed to have a Jewish secretary or night watchman now. And then, a few days later, yet another new law: professionals – physicians, lawyers, engineers, dentists – are no longer allowed to practice their professions. Then the yellow star law, then the law restricting the food they are allowed to consume, the elegantly named 'law to limit the supply of foodstuffs to the Jews.' Then the law forbidding the Jews to keep shops or restaurants, to own factories, workshops or farms. We cannot keep pace with all these laws and regulations, and quite simply, we cannot see any point to them. But now, all these laws have in effect been abolished by the imprisonment of all the Jews in a ghetto. We have examined the text of these laws and have come to the conclusion that in the final instance they remove the right to work from this category of citizen. And removal of the right to work means nothing less than removal of the right to life –'

'Oh, it's hardly that serious,' muttered notary public Zeleznay. 'They have tidy sums of money, which they've accumulated over the years.'

'What does money matter in the face of eternity?' said Pritko, unexpectedly.

'Some have money, others don't,' continued the judge. 'The majority have nothing. They lived hand to mouth. I know them from cases brought before the court. And those that do have money will spend it all sooner or later, if they are not able to work.'

'It's their own fault,' said the notary public, eating a chunk of bread topped by a thick slice of toasted bacon fat. 'They were too stuck-up, showing off their wealth.'

Mrs Zelaznay, the notary public's wife, interjected: 'Their women walked around dolled up with jewellery and dresses ordered from Vienna and Paris. Just the other Saturday, one of Blumenthal's daughters-in-law went for a stroll with her husband wearing a cherry-red Chinese silk dress, with flounces and a gilt belt. She looked frightful!'

'Not at all. I think it suited her,' said Mrs Daoben. 'But anyway, I assure you, Mrs Zeleznay, she doesn't wear dresses from Vienna or Paris, but has them made by the same seamstress I go to. My seamstress is not at all expensive, I can give you her address, if you like.'

'But they're as stubborn as mules,' said the notary public. 'Before they were taken to the ghetto, I spoke to my good neighbour Mr

Blumenthal and offered to buy his house and garden, since they were going to be confiscated anyway, and who knows who will get his hands on them. He adamantly refused!'

'And when he returned, you would have given him back the property?'

'When he returned? How could he return? Is that why they were removed from their houses, so that they could return? Don't be so naïve, Dr Daoben. They will be taken somewhere… How should I know where? Maybe to Palestine…'

'Everything that happens is because of the stars!' interrupted Pritko. 'The position of the stars dictates the Jews' being taken to the ghetto, our excursion, the catching and eating of trout, Blumenthal's daughter-in-law's Chinese silk dress, everything, everything. Nothing is taken away from anybody, nothing is given to anybody. Nobody deserves anything and nobody is guilty of anything…'

The others laughed. Judge Daoben gave his rather ironic assent: 'Bravo, Pritko! Perhaps you are right… Ultimately I really do think you are right. It seems to me that the stars now say that it is time for us to go home.'

The women cleared away the meal and the company set off down the valley, towards the town.

Ernst emerged from the bushes, devastated. His parents, brothers, sisters-in-law, the whole family was shut up in the ghetto, while he roamed free in the mountains. And that neighbour of theirs, the honourable notary public Mr Zeleznay… so jovial, always smiling whenever he spoke to his father, and there he was, attempting to lay hands on the family home. The Blumenthal family could be packed off to Palestine or the devil knows where, as far as he was concerned. These were the neighbours they had lived next to for so many years? What kind of world was this? How had things deteriorated like this in the space of just a few months? Ernst could find no answer. Could the answer be in the stars, as that madman Pritko said?

Night had fallen and Ernst went back to the house. He crossed the stile and climbed up into the hayloft of Ionu Stan's barn. But he was unable to go to sleep. He tossed and turned in his nest, and he was unable to smell the moist hay. What was happening to his family in the crowded ghetto? How did they live? Did they have food to eat? And there he was, walking at liberty in the forest, gazing avidly at the green grass, the herbs, the thistles, the trees, the ants, the butterflies, the gnats. It was utterly ridiculous. And sad. Sad and ridiculous.

The next day was a Wednesday, the weekly market day in Sighet. Ionu usually went down into the town, to sell sheep's cheese and two or three hens, to buy flour, cooking oil, salt and other household essentials. Ernst asked him to try to find out about his family. And if he managed to talk to one of his family, to ask what he, Ernst, could do. Should he come down from his hiding place and join them in the ghetto? Ernst felt that the idea was absurd. The gates of the ghetto were guarded by gendarmes, and nobody was allowed to enter without special permission. And who would try to enter and expose himself to unpleasantness and even unforeseen dangers? In his desperation, Ernst nonetheless asked Ionu to try, but to be cautious.

Ernst did not have the slightest hope that his host would succeed in the mission with which he had entrusted him. But what else could he do? His helplessness made him desperate.

Things do not always turn out the way we imagine. Ionu Stan succeeded, and he did so beyond all expectation. Nor had he had to expose himself to danger, even to approach the gates of the ghetto. In the market people had been talking about the events of the day and it was rumoured that the Jews from the ghetto, including the gentlemen – the doctors, lawyers, merchants – had been taken to the railway depot, where they were made to load coal into locomotive tenders.

Ionu went to the station, crossed thirteen pairs of rails, and reached the depot. He saw there some hundred men, most of them wearing town clothes, some of them even wearing white shirts and ties, lugging in pairs large baskets of coal and emptying them into the tenders. They were not very closely guarded. Those gentlemen were not so witless as to attempt to flee. And where would they have fled anyway? Their houses were sealed, their families were in the ghetto, and so the handful of policemen on guard stood in a group, smoking and chatting. But how could Ionu find out if anybody from the Blumenthal family was there? A brother of his neighbour Vasile Vlaşin worked at the depot. Teodor Vlaşin was his name, and he was a locomotive mechanic. Teodor Vlaşin looked at the list of Jews who had been brought there to work, which list he had to sign to confirm those present, and he found the name Blumenthal. Jacob Blumenthal. It was Ernst's second-eldest brother. His eldest brother Mauriciu was much older and too frail to lug heavy baskets of coal, and so he had remained in the ghetto, where he had to sweep the streets.

Teodor Vlaşin summoned Blumenthal to clean the locomotive cabin. And there he met Ionu Son of the Trustworthy One. Ionu told him that his brother Ernst was worried, that he did not know what to do, that he was thinking about coming down from the mountains of his own free will and giving himself up, so that he could be shut up in the ghetto with the rest of the family.

'God forbid!' exclaimed Jacob. 'Don't let him do such at thing! Tell him we are fine, that we have a place where we can sleep. Under the present circumstances, that is almost a good thing. We have to wait until the storm passes. And when it does, it is of the utmost necessity that at least one member of the family be at liberty…'

Ionu Son of the Trustworthy One told Ernst everything he had talked of with his brother Jacob.

Ernst's worry was not allayed, but he had no choice: he would have to live with it. And he would have to live with the fear and the question to which he found no answer: How had things come to this?

In the valleys and on the hills of Solovan, Agriş, Meia and Siheiu there was great rejoicing. Eudochia, the eldest daughter of Ionu Stan Son of the Trustworthy One, was marrying Vasile Vlaşin, the son of Vasile Vlaşin, Ionu's closest neighbour, whose house was some three kilometres away.

Although the young couple had known each other since they were children and had long had an understanding, the betrothal and wedding were held according to the ancient customs of Maramureş.

One morning, a close relative, Vasile Vlaşin's brother Teodor, the locomotive mechanic from Sighet, arrived in Ionu's farmyard and solemnly asked: 'Do you have any hay, after-grass or straw for sale?'

Ionu and Ileanu came out onto the porch: 'We have hay and after-grass for sale.'

If they had answered that they had only straw for sale, the relative would not have then ventured to ask for the girl. These were roundabout preliminaries, designed to avoid a refusal, which would have offended, perhaps for a lifetime, the suitor's parents.

The two youngsters met and decided on a betrothal day, when they would exchange rings, and on a wedding day. They were a handsome couple. She was tall, with chestnut hair and the green eyes of a wild cat. She was hardworking and cheerful, like her mother. He was strong, skilled at cutting wood in the sawmill, and his bearing was as straight and proud as a fir tree in the forest.

All the valleys and hills were in ferment. The two families had relatives everywhere. The friends of the groom were busy making the marriage banner, a pole cut from a young pine tree. From it were hung scarves of different colours, so that they would shine like a rainbow when the flag bearer whirled the pole. Eudochia's friends were busy with the bridal garland. The parents and relatives were preparing food for the feast.

The wedding guests, all wearing colourful festive garments, descended to the small wooden church in Sihei, where the ceremony was held, after which they climbed back up the hill, with the large banner and lesser banners, with musicians playing, and with the whole procession dancing and calling out jocularly, teasing each other.

The wedding procession arrived at the groom's house, where they danced and feasted, before moving on to the bride's house, where they ate and danced till midnight.

Ernst watched the merriment from a hiding place, not wishing anybody to see him.

'Look how the world is made up,' Ernst said to himself. 'One part suffers, the other dances and makes merry.'

Just three days after Ernst made this banal observation, the young husband of the beautiful Eudochia, Vasile Vlașin, received the order to enlist in the army. He was not placed in a regular unit; he was not issued with a rifle. He was assigned to a labour brigade, with picks and shovels, and taken to dig earthworks and bunkers on the border at Iașina.

6

On the morning of 16 May 1944, Ernst woke up abruptly in his bed of moist hay in the loft of Ionu Stan's barn.

He thought he had heard a noise rising from the town, a strange hum made up of words and cries, mingled with harsh orders. Was it a dream? No, the sound persisted, perhaps more faintly than during sleep, but even so, it could still be heard up there on the slope of Agriş Hill.

Gripped by a presentiment, given that down in the town so many things had happened since he had come to the forest, Ernst took his binoculars and quickly went to the fire watchtower.

Along three streets moved three columns of people, escorted by gendarmes armed to the teeth. Women, men, the elderly, children, each carrying a heavy bundle, suitcases, pillows, pots and pans wrapped up in bed sheets. People pale and silent. Angry people perorating left and right. People in wheelchairs. Women weeping in unison with their children.

The ghetto was being evacuated. They had begun with Tanners Street, and then moved on to Autumn Street and the brickworks. All three columns, moving along three different streets, were heading for Sighet railway station.

'Where are they taking them now?' wondered Ernst, thoroughly frightened. 'Where are they taking them and all their chattels, on those cattle cars waiting for them at the station?'

In the town not one window was open. Not one door. Not another soul could be seen in the streets.

The evacuation of the ghetto lasted five days. Twelve thousand peaceful citizens were transported in cattle cars to an unknown destination.

Ernst was in despair.

But on the second day Ionu Stan came from town with encouraging news. It was rumoured that the Jews were being taken beyond the Danube, where they would work on large estates and farms, to replace the young peasants who had gone to the front.

Ernst felt calmer.

But calm in such times is fleeting.

The next day, after the third transport left Sighet, Vasile Vlașin and his wife Dana came to the house of Ionu for supper. Vlașin's wife was a beautiful woman, rather plump, with a smiling face, as swarthy as a gypsy's. She was cradling her baby, a lad of three months.

Vlașin, her husband, was furious. Why had the Russians stopped at the Carpathian bend, beyond Iașina? Why had they advanced on Jassy and Bucharest? And his son, three days after his wedding, now had to dig trenches and build bunkers there in Iașina. They were all waiting for the Russians, although God knows what joy they would bring, after they liberated them… It was said that they built collective farms everywhere and you had to queue with a canteen for food.

Later, hesitantly, looking Ionu in the eye, Vlașin recounted that his brother Teodor had been the train driver on the third transport. In keeping with the rumours, he had expected the train to head south, to the region beyond the Danube, where the landowners and the barons had their estates. But the locomotive had been sent north.

'North?' asked Ernst in stupefaction.

'And it went to the border of German-occupied Poland, where Teodor was replaced with another mechanic, a Pole or a German, one of the two. And an escort of German soldiers in black uniforms took over the train.'

Where had they been taken? What would happen to them there? How would they live? Ernst asked himself, falling into silent despair once more.

It was enough to drive you insane.

What ferment in town, in the valley below, and what tranquillity up here!

Ionu, Vasile Vlaşin and others from the mountain villages returned from town with some very strange news. In Sighet, on the walls and fences, posters had appeared, inscribed in large letters: 'Public execution.' The poster informed the town's citizens that on Friday, on the day of the monthly fair, three Russian partisans captured in the Carpathian Mountains were to be lined up against a wall in the marketplace and shot. Using radios and by means of fires lit at night in certain places, they had been transmitting signals and messages, guiding Soviet transport aeroplanes to Tito's Yugoslav partisans. They had been tried by court martial and were to be publicly executed, to serve as an example and a warning to the town's citizens.

From his watchtower, which had once belonged to the fire brigade, Ernst watched the whole scene through his binoculars. A large crowd of people had gathered around a wall on one side of the marketplace. The vendors had left their stalls unattended, just so that they could get closer and have a better view.

Some officials and leading townsmen arrived, wearing black suits, white shirts and black ties, along with some high-ranking officers, their chests full of gleaming decorations. They stationed themselves to the left of the wall.

The firing squad waited with the butts of their rifles resting by their feet.

Finally, the partisans were brought out, handcuffed, and were stood up against the wall. The one in the middle was very tall and thin, the one to his left was short and fat, and the one to his right was so small and puny that the wind could have blown him away.

Ernst watched through his powerful binoculars. He could not make out the people's faces, but he could see very well their movements, like in a puppet play with a cast of tiny actors with aged faces.

An officer read from a large sheet of paper, and then another officer gave the command. The firing squad raised their rifles and

Ernst heard a volley of faint pops. Or perhaps he only thought he could hear them.

The tall, thin partisan doubled up and fell face forward. The fat one on his right slid down with his back against the wall and remained sitting there, as if enjoying the shade. The third, the puny one, fell sideways and lay with his head propped against a stone.

The crowd began to run away, as if gripped by terror, the men were making the sign of the cross, the women were weeping, wiping their eyes with the corners of their headscarves.

The next day, very early in the morning, Ernst emerged from his bed of hay, went to the stream to wash his face and hands, and then set off towards Meia Hill, where he had a pleasant hiding place, a glade with lush silky grass, surrounded by sheltering nut bushes.

Silence! Only the hum of the gnats and the chirping of the birds could be heard. 'The air is good, the water is good!' Ernst said to himself, quoting a saying from a story he had heard from his hiking companion Judge Rudolf Daoben:

Soon after the end of the First World War, the Romanian Government decided to colonise the Banat with Romanian peasants. Up until the collapse of the Austro-Hungarian Empire and Romania's annexation of the territory, the Banat had been peopled almost entirely with German peasants. Who else would the government ask to come to the Banat if not peasants from Maramureş, whose land was sparse and mountainous, whose soil was poor and hard to work, and whose families were numerous? In the Banat they would have the rich soil of the plains and bountiful harvests. The Prefect of Maramureş assembled a number of the wiser, more prosperous peasants and made the proposal.

The peasants were silent.

'Well, what do you say? Does it suit you to move to the Banat?'

The prefect was almost certain of a positive answer.

But the peasants were silent.

'Why don't you say anything, good people? I've made you an offer you can't refuse!'

'Well,' said one of the peasants, 'no offence, mister prefect, but we don't know anything, we haven't seen anything…'

They are right, said the prefect to himself. And straight away he formed a delegation of peasants to go and see the land and how the people there lived. He was convinced that they would come back persuaded.

The delegation left, roamed the length and breadth of the Banat, and came back home. The prefect assembled them in the functions hall of the prefecture and asked them:

'Well, good people, did you see?'

'We saw.'

The prefect, who was from somewhere near Pitești, saw that he would have to drag the words out of those mountain men with tongs.

'Is the land good?'

'Good, mister prefect.'

'Is the harvest rich?'

'It's rich.'

'Then have you decided to move?'

'No, mister prefect.'

The prefect was left perplexed.

'Why not?'

'Because here the water is good and the air is good.'

And the peasants did not move.

Ernst was in a good mood. He smiled at the story, he smiled at the good air and the good water of those mountains, and he continued on his way to Meia, without a care.

He was in the wide, open valley, not far from the lightning-blasted tree.

All of a sudden Ernst came to a stop, as if struck by lightning, like the tree in front of him. Two gendarmes were coming down from

Meia Hill, with cockerel feathers in their caps and carbines over their shoulders. Their heavy black boots trampled the lush green grass, marching in regulation rhythm.

'It's all over! No more peace and quiet in the woods and valleys!' said Ernst to himself.

He was hidden from view by the lightning-blasted tree in front of him. But the gendarmes were approaching. He had to hide himself quickly. He could go neither left nor right. To the right, there were at least two hundred metres to the forest on the hill. To the left, there were at least three hundred metres to the spinneys in the valley. Nor could he go back the way he came, because there would be no cover once he moved away from the hollow oak. Whichever way he went he would be in range of the gendarmes' rifles.

The gendarmes were nearing. Struck by an idea, Ernst quickly slipped inside the hollow of the tree. He breathed a sigh of relief. The tall, burly gendarmes passed by the tree, treading the soft, yielding grass as they marched in step.

'They're not such big heroes when they think nobody else is looking,' observed Ernst.

He had overhead them talking as they passed: 'We could end up shot in the back,' said one.

'I wouldn't put it past the partisans,' said the other.

Ernst watched their broad backs moving into the distance before vanishing over the horizon. He made to climb out of the hollow. He was unable to. He tried to move his right arm outside, but something obstructed his shoulder, probably a knot in the tree. He tried to move his left arm, but was again unable to. Ernst began to laugh out loud. There was nothing for him to fear: 'I got inside easily and now I can't get out. What is going on?' He tried to get out sideways. He was unable to, and merely scraped his left shoulder blade. What was this? Ernst couldn't understand. Or maybe only his fear of the gendarmes had caused him, without his realising it, to find the right angle to be able to climb inside. He felt his legs growing numb. He began to struggle desperately. He vigorously moved his fingers and toes. With no result. He was a prisoner in the hollow tree. What was wrong with him? Ernst became serious. It could be weeks before anybody passed this way. He would die of hunger and thirst. They would find him decomposing, after who knows how long an interval. Ernst burst into tears. He then calmed down a little.

Ernst felt an emptiness in his mind. He was no longer capable of thinking about anything. And he fell asleep there in the hollow of the lightning-blasted oak, like a heavy stone that could not be turned over.

He slept like that for a few hours, until dusk, when the sun shone a few playful rays into the hollow. They tickled him in his sleep. They woke him and Ernst found himself ejected out of the hollow. Smoothly, painlessly, without resistance, Ernst slid from the hollow and quickly crawled away on all fours, filled with indescribable elation. He walked on all fours like a dog and barked at the top of his voice. That was what he wanted, what he liked.

Then, he tumbled around in the soft grass. He rolled for a few hundred metres. Ernst was happy. He did not care about the thunder rumbling across the sky, nor about the rain that suddenly started to pour down, nor the flashes of lightning, nor the darkened sky, which hastened the onset of night.

Soaked to the skin by the warm rain, he reached the hayloft of Ionu Stan's barn, where he kept his knapsack with a change of clothes. He was just about to change his shirt when he heard unusual sounds from the house: shouting, quarrelling, a child crying. What was going on? Ionu's house was always so peaceful. He was a gentle, taciturn man, and when he spoke it was in a soft, singsong way, he never raised his voice.

Ernst went up to the house and looked through the little window of the main room. He beheld a strange and desolate scene. Ionu, who had never in his life drunk more than a small tot of plum schnapps, was blind drunk. He was shouting, but his words were slurred and

Ernst could not understand a single syllable. He was brandishing an axe, at his family or at the air around him – it was unclear which. The children, Adilina and Ionuț, were bawling by the stove, and Ileana, vital and resourceful, was trying to quiet them.

'We'll see what we can do tomorrow! Calm down, Ionu!'

'I won't! I'll kill him, so that he won't talk… With this axe I'll kill him… I don't want you to be kicked out of house and home… A spectacle for everybody to see!' shouted Ionu and reached for the bottle of plum schnapps on the table. Ileana took it from his hand.

'Enough! That's enough! We'll see what we can do tomorrow… Now go to bed!' she said.

'I can't. Go to bed, first I have to get rid of him…'

And holding the axe he went outside.

Ernst now understood that Ionu meant him. But why this change? Up until then he had been a guest, albeit a paying guest. And they had got on together very well. Ionu had even brought him news from town, when something happened, and all of a sudden things had taken this unexpected and inexplicable turn. Now he was coming to kill him with the axe.

Ernst waited for him by the door of the porch. Ionu opened the door and in the light that streamed out of the house, he saw his guest. They looked each other in the eye for a few moments, and then Ernst quickly grabbed the wrist of the hand in which Ionu was holding the axe. Held limply, the axe fell from Ionu's hand. Then, Ionu fell too, collapsing on the floorboards of the porch, where he began to cry like a child. Ileana and Ernst lifted him up, took off his frieze jerkin and trousers, and put him to bed on his trunk, where he slept like a new-born baby.

As soon as Ionu fell asleep, Ernst discovered the reason for his host's strange and incomprehensible behaviour.

After everyone else in the house was asleep, Ileana turned down the oil lamp and in the semi-darkness, she told the tale in a low voice.

'A few days ago, in the evening, a man dressed in peasant clothes came to Vasile Vlașin's house and said his name was Petru Hoduț, and that he was from the village of Teceu, on his way to Sighet to buy a milk cow. He had taken a shortcut through the Solovan Mountains and before he could reach Sighet night had fallen and he didn't want to continue in the dark, as he might get lost. That was why he asked for shelter there overnight. Vasile Vlașin, keeping to the custom of Maramureș, would never refuse to receive a tired and hungry guest in his house. Vlașin's wife, Dana, didn't like the look of that guest and in the larder, where Vlașin had gone to fetch some milk and cheese, she timidly told him: 'Vasile, I don't like that man.'

"Why'

"I don't know.'

They had given the man shelter, fed him, and made a bed for him in the room on the right, by the porch.

In the morning, the guest rose at the same time as the rest of the house. Vlașin had seven children. The youngest, an unweaned babe of five months, was screaming for the breast at the break of day.

The guest asked Vlașin for a razor, so that he wouldn't turn up at the cattle mart in Sighet unshaven. Vlașin climbed up on a stool, since the razor was kept on a beam by the ceiling. He gave the guest the razor and a piece of shaving soap. After that, the man sat down at the table, in a good mood, and laughed and joked with the family. He praised his host for the good maize porridge he served him that morning.

Dana became more and more disquieted. Peasants don't talk like that, she thought. But she didn't say anything. Before leaving, the guest wanted to pay, but Vlașin, noticing his jerkin and trousers were patched, refused to take a penny from him.

The man thanked his host and bade him farewell, with the traditional: 'Christ is risen.'

'Truly He is risen,' replied Vlașin.

The visit took place on a Monday. The Tuesday and the Wednesday were quiet, but that Thursday evening, three guests turned up at Vlașin's house: an officer and two gendarmes with cockerel feathers in their caps.

'Recognise me?' asked the officer, elegant in his pressed *honvéd* army uniform and shining boots.

'I recognise you,' said Vlașin. 'You're Petru Hoduț, the peasant from Teceu.'

The officer frowned.

'No! I am Captain Deloczy Istvan of the counterespionage service.'

'You didn't tell us that, captain, sir, otherwise we would have regaled you better.'

The officer was rather taken aback. He didn't know how to conduct himself in a peasant's house late in the evening. He began to arrange to question the family.

He lined up Vlașin's six children by the wall. He ordered Vlașin's daughter-in-law, Eudochia, who was staying there while her husband was doing his military service, to make sure the children kept quiet. The children gazed wide-eyed during this strange ceremony.

He made Dana, holding the baby, stand to the right of Vlașin, who had remained standing like a statue in the middle of the room. Vlașin was unable to understand what serious crime he had committed for a captain of counterespionage and two gendarmes to enter his house like that.

One gendarme stood guard at the door, as if one of them might try to escape, and the other sat at the corner of the large table, with a pen and a sheet of paper, to write the *procès verbal*.

Captain Doloczy sat solemnly at the table and began the interrogation.

'Vlașin Vasile, did you provide shelter to a stranger in your house without notifying the authorities?'

'I didn't know anybody had to be notified. It's our ancestral custom to give shelter to strangers.'

'Never mind the ancestral customs!' shouted the officer in annoyance. 'Answer yes or no!'

'Then, yes! I gave shelter to you!'

'You also gave him a razor so he could shave! It's up there, on the beam by the ceiling.' He pointed out the place to the gendarme by the door. 'Take it, it's *corpus delicti*. You helped that stranger alter his appearance.'

'I didn't help him do anything, officer, sir. The man wanted to shave.'

Then, after a pause, Vlașin went on: 'Perhaps you'll allow me to fetch a lawyer from Sighet.'

'There's a *statarium* in the land, a state of siege, didn't you know?' the captain barked. 'We have the enemy in front of us, the partisans behind, and you want us to listen to endless legal quibbling…'

The officer was furious. He looked at the gendarme writing the *procès verbal* next to him, who was struggling to keep up.

'Why do you write so slowly?'

'It has to be legible, captain, sir!'

The officer grabbed the dossier, noisily shut it, and gave the order to leave. Vlașin and his wife with her babe in arms were shoved out of the front door, followed by Captain Deloczy and the two gendarmes, who lit the way with storm lanterns. The children were left behind, in the care of Eudochia.

They descended to the wooden bridge over the Iza. Two vehicles were waiting for them on the other side of the river: a van and a jeep. They set out and three hours later arrived in Kassa, a large town, which served as the regional military base and where all the courts martial sat.

The next morning, Vasile Vlașin was brought before the court martial. His wife was also brought, separately. Vlașin came before the judges with his ancestral law, and Captain Deloczy Istvan with his state of siege. Wishing to impress the court, the captain, who was testifying as a witness, launched into a passionate speech: 'The Carpathians are swarming with partisans!' cried the officer, with pathos.

'Swarming! I haven't seen a single partisan,' thought Vlașin.

'Two weeks ago, three partisans were captured and executed in Sighet. These Romanians give them shelter. And not only do they shelter them and give them food, drink and warm beds to keep them strong, they also help them to disguise themselves, to alter their appearance. Here is the razor the accused gave me, so that I would look decent… Honourable court martial, an example has to be made, so that these people will no longer endanger us behind our front line, so that they will no longer threaten our army, which is engaged in such a fierce struggle against the Bolshevik enemy…'

An example was made. Vasile Vlașin was sentenced to hang. The execution was to take place the next morning. Things were done in a hurry at the court martial there in Kassa. The queues were long and the trials were short.

On the way to his execution, and beneath the gallows pole, Vlașin behaved calmly, merely repeating over and over again: 'I did nothing, nothing, nothing, nothing, nothing…'

His wife Dana watched that hallucinatory ceremony with her eyes starting from her head. And when the chair was taken from beneath Vlașin's feet, she let out a piercing cry: 'No-o-o-o-o-o-o…' And then she fell down in a faint.

They brought her round, gave her hot tea and food for herself and the baby, and then they sent her back home, with the order to roam the mountains, to go to Sihei and Meia, to Agriș and Solovan, to the villages and houses, and to tell what she had seen.

Having heard Ileana's account, in the dim lamplight, Ernst decided to leave Ionu Stan's house immediately and not to come near it again. Nor would he approach any other house in those hills. Ileana told him that from time to time he would find in a place known to them alone some potatoes, a maize loaf, raw cabbage, apples.

After the execution of his father, Vasile Vlașin, the son, was not discharged from the army and nor was he given home leave. Rather, he continued to work in the labour brigade, with pick and shovel, reinforcing the border at Iașina.

Eudochia, the wife of the younger Vasile, remained in the house of her in-laws, to look after the seven children, including the babe in arms, after Dana returned that evening. Obeying the order she was given in Kassa, by day she roamed the villages, telling her story.

Ernst saw her once, when she passed the clearing on Meia Hill; he espied her from behind the branches. She looked like a wild woman of the woods from the stories to frighten children. He saw the wild expression of that gentle woman, in contrast with the dead eyes, which no longer seemed to see anybody. Her swarthy gypsy face was more beautiful than ever, and her dishevelled, tangled hair, once so black, seemed to burn red and blue in the rays of the setting sun.

She passed slowly, with her babe in arms, and sang softly in a reedy, childlike voice:

Proudly ring the bells,
Now deep, now high,
For our parting's nigh…

The local peasants, along with their animals, divined that the coming winter, the winter of 1944, would be harsh. Preparing for hibernation, architecture student Ernst Blumenthal made himself an all but invisible hut on the slope of Meia Hill, or rather a den of branches and leaves.

But one September day, a rumour of great joy spread through the Solovan, Agriș, Meia, and Sihei mountains: Sighet had been liberated. The Soviet Army was in the town. The Russians had not made a frontal attack on the reinforced border at Iașina, but had taken a large detour, coming down through Jassy in Moldavia, and then coming back up through Transylvania. The German and Hungarian armies, in danger of being encircled and annihilated, had been forced to retreat through Maramureș, without firing a shot.

Ernst tossed his things in his knapsack and set off down the valley. He floated rather than walked, as if borne on the breeze, which blew from behind. He went by paths and shortcuts known only to him. At the wooden bridge over the Iza there was no sentinel. He breathed in the fresh morning air. Having been tensed for so long, now he could relax at last. Yes, Ernst felt that henceforth a different world would come, a different and better order for people and mankind. He felt that he could breathe freely, think freely, feel freely, and speak freely…

His street was quiet, empty. There was not a soul to be seen. The gate of his house was open. Ernst was amazed. Somebody had broken the large red seals on the front door. In his parents' bedroom he found a Soviet soldier. The soldier, who was quite old and had one eye missing, looked at the peasant before him without surprise. He rested his automatic rifle against the bed and took some warm flannel long johns from the cupboard, measuring them against himself to see whether they fit. He took two pairs and said to Ernst: 'Take whatever you need. *Voina*.' There's a war on, in other words. And then he left.

He's right, Ernst said to himself. *Voina*. There's a war on, it's cold, and winter is coming. The soldier had a long way to go, as far as Germany, maybe even all the way to Berlin.

Ernst felt happy inside. Soon the war would be over, his parents and brothers would come back, and life would continue as before. He took off his peasant clothes, put on town clothes, and went out into town.

There were very few people on the streets of the town, mostly old folk and women with bags and baskets. People did not know what liberation would bring, what the new government would be, what it would look like, up close, as it were. And they emerged from their houses fearfully.

His soul bursting, Ernst wandered the town's main streets. He passed the Palace of Culture and remembered the trap into which he had fallen with the bedsteads and mattresses for the German soldiers. And he felt happy. He had finished with all that. There would be law and order in the town now, the same as in the past.

'*Stoi!* Stop!' a loud voice shouted behind him. Ernst turned around. A soviet soldier, on guard at the gate of the Palace of Culture, was pointing his automatic rifle at his chest.

'Inside!' ordered the soldier. Ernst felt an increasing tension between them.

'Why should I go inside?' asked Ernst, very surprised.

The soldier did not understand what that stammering local was saying, but he could see that he was hesitating, and so he shouted loudly, brandishing his rifle: 'Inside!'

Ernst went inside. He saw black before his eyes. Inside were a few hundred men in tattered Wehrmacht and SS uniforms with the shoulder tabs torn off. Some of them had suppurating wounds on their arms and legs. A few were in civilian clothes: some of them suspected of having abandoned their uniforms before falling prisoner, others from the administration.

The prisoners were lined up for morning roll call and to receive their coffee. Ernst was made to join the line. He looked out of the corner of his eyes at the prisoner on his left: a thin, lanky old man. He looked to his right and felt an unpleasant thrill: it was a young officer, in a shabby black uniform, who looked like the one who had made him pick up bits of straw from the broad stairs of that very palace. But he was not sure.

What was he doing there? Why had they made him come inside? Was he trapped in another hollow tree? Life sometimes has all kinds of hollow trees in store for the unsuspecting. Ernst tried to escape once more; he spoke to the soldiers, almost shouting at them.

They threatened him with their guns, but he did not care. The soldiers could not understand a word he was saying.

'Me to the commandant,' said Ernst, and pointed at his mouth. 'I want to speak to the commandant in charge of the prisoners.'

The thought of ending up by mistake in a prisoner of war camp after the war was over was unbearable.

The business reached the ears of the commandant, who invited Ernst into his office. It was an office only in a manner of speaking. In fact, it was furnished with a green baize table and two creaking chairs. In one corner was an old sideboard, which looked like it might fall to pieces at any moment.

The prisoners were only passing through the town.

When he entered the commandant's office, Ernst shuddered. He stood no chance, he said to himself. The commandant, whom the soldiers called Major Nikolayev, had a fierce face with a large black moustache and bulging eyes. He had a scar over his left eyebrow. On the table in front of him was a bottle containing a red liquid, probably rum, and a full glass.

With a severe gesture, the commandant signalled him to sit. He understood a little German and told Ernst to speak. Ernst told him that he had been roped in without having done anything. He was not a Nazi or an SS man. He was not even a soldier of the Wehrmacht. He had lived in the town for decades, his parents and grandparents and great-grandparents had lived there. He was a Jew and he had hidden in the mountains from the Nazis.

'I understand you! I understand you very well!' said Major Nikolayev, and his face softened.

Ernst breathed a sigh of relief. It just went to show that you shouldn't judge a man by how he looked.

Major Nikolayev stood up, took a large glass from the disintegrating sideboard, and put it in front of Ernst. He filled it with rum.

'Drink!' said the officer. 'It will do you good.'

Ernst was happy. He was sure the major was going to release him.

But the commandant was in no hurry. After a moment's thought, he asked: 'Are you married?'

'No,' answered Ernst.

'I have a wife and four children.'

The major took from the top pocket of his uniform a crumpled scrap of paper.

'I have here a *prepuska*. I have to turn over seven hundred prisoners. What do you think will happen if I arrive with fewer than that? They will demote me, send me to prison for years and years. Failure to do one's duty in wartime. Do you understand what that means? The war will be over and I, the father of four children, will be in prison, after serving for five years in the war and being wounded three times… Do you understand?'

The whole of that night, Ernst did not sleep a wink. He wept silently, with his fist crammed in his mouth.

In the morning, the column of seven hundred prisoners was taken to the loading ramp of Sighet Station.

At eight in the morning, on the dot, the train, its metal creaking, lumbered into motion, heading east.

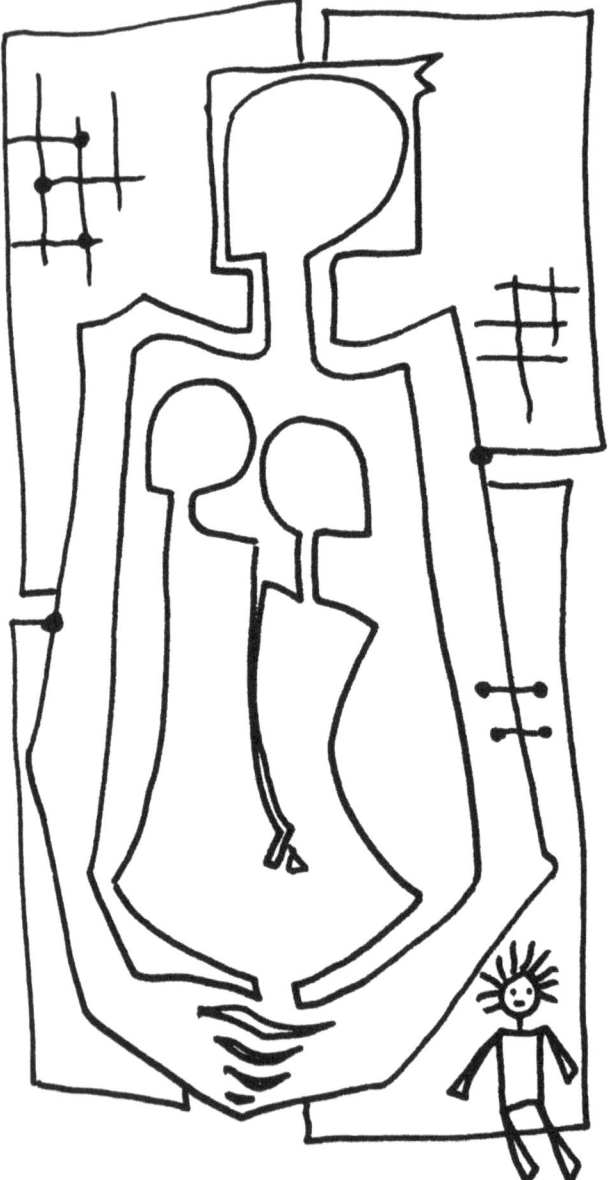

THE RAG DOLL

They were sitting at a small round table in the restaurant of a large international airport. At intervals, through the glass wall in front of them, big silver aeroplanes could be seen landing on the white cement strips or taking off and vanishing into the distance.

The woman was absentmindedly warming her fingertips on her steaming cup of coffee, while the little girl ate a large portion of red and green ice cream, raspberry and pineapple flavour, taking the spoon out of her mouth and sticking out her tongue to catch the melting droplets that ran down the side of the glass.

'Behave, Evuni!' said her mother gently.

Eva-Magdalena was the little girl's name, but her mother called her Evuni. And that was what everybody else in the family called her, and everybody on the street, everybody in her third-year class in primary school. The little girl had dark chestnut hair, like her father's, long silky hair tied in ponytails that her mother couldn't bear to cut, even though ponytails had long since gone out of fashion, and she had clear blue eyes, like her mother's. Hanna Kamin, the girl's mother, was a woman still beautiful, with light blond hair, which quite well disguised the few white strands at her temples; her face was fine-featured, the skin smooth, luminous, almost without wrinkles. It was a beauty that didn't leap out at you, a beauty that you noticed only after looking at it for a while. But looking at her luminous blue-eyed face, nobody would have been able to imagine that that small, delicate woman had lost, one by one, in the strangest and most various circumstances, her parents, her husband, her eldest daughter, her home, her home town, the village where she had lived for so many years… Everything. Almost everything. All she had left were two suitcases of clothes and underwear, two aeroplane tickets, and that little girl, Evuni, now licking melted ice cream from the side of her glass.

'Evuni, what are you doing? It's not nice…'

She had lost everything, or almost everything, for the sake of a lie that she had never spoken aloud and which she had found herself living without her realising it…

It seemed to her that it had all been nothing but a dream. A hallucinatory dream from which she had only just awoken. The only reality was that steaming cup of coffee in front of her, the child who kept poking out her tongue to lick the red and green ice cream, raspberry and pineapple flavour, that international airport with its thronging people and their luggage, the large silver aeroplanes that could be seen through the glass wall of the restaurant, landing on the white strips of the aerodrome or elegantly taking off and vanishing into the distance, the metallic, slightly distorted voice of the megaphone that made her give a start: 'Flight number 405 will be departing in ten minutes… Passengers are invited…'

They were in transit through that huge aerodrome. They had come from the north and had to make a transfer before travelling south, where an aged aunt was waiting for them, the aunt who had once given her a strange rag doll… But when had it been?

There was no longer any before, and who knows what would come after? No matter what was to come, no matter how many unexpected events might arise, she would be ready. In her soul, joy mingled with the fear of what was to come, and fear with the joy that what had come before was now the past, since everything in this world passes. The range of her moods had narrowed and strangely coalesced, making her more hardened, more impervious to blows and surprises. What she had made for herself in life was not a home but adventure, which sits well with youth, and perhaps it sat well with her too (how many times had she not smiled happily at her reflection in the mirror?) but now that she was approaching her fifties…

Yes, the only reality was now that airport full of people and their luggage, that booming, distorted voice from the megaphone that made her give a start – any minute now they would be announcing the flight: 'Flight 707 will be departing in ten minutes… passengers are invited…' The only reality was the steaming coffee in front of her and the little girl poking her tongue out to lick the red and green ice cream.

'Evuni, what are you doing? How many times do I have to tell you?'

Before that, it had all been nothing but a dream. A hallucinatory dream. What had been before?

She had had a happy childhood. Her parents' only daughter, after she came into the world they gave her everything. They worked for her, they rested for her, they breathed for her, they prayed for her, they lived for her. Her mother, small, thin, with a long, slender face, an industrious woman – that is how she remembered her – had a large black comb with a handle and while her mother was in the kitchen, the little girl would sit for hours combing her long blond hair in front of the mirror. When her mother came from the kitchen, wiping her hands on the white apron that covered her black skirt, she would comb her daughter's hair for her once more, making a perfect parting down the middle and tying it in two plaits with a red ribbon at the end.

She had no shortage of toys. A large doll with red cheeks and lemon-yellow hair used to close its round, glassy blue eyes when she laid it on its back and it would make a thin groan when she pressed its tummy. She also had a complete bedroom set for the doll: a table with four chairs, a wardrobe for clothes and underwear, and a cot with a soft mattress, all of which she kept in one corner of her room. But little Hanna was very aggrieved, because the big, plump doll with the lemon-yellow hair and glassy blue eyes would not fit in the cot, which was too small. The doll's legs dangled outside the blanket. Seeing it like that, with its legs dangling, she had felt sorry for it at first, but then she grew sick of it and couldn't bear to look at it anymore.

She went on being aggrieved until the day she received another doll, a rag doll, which fit in the cot perfectly. It was given to her by Esta, which is to say, Aunt Esther, one of her father's younger sisters, a very beautiful girl, with short glossy black hair, which she wore swept back, like a boy, and who had lively, restless dark eyes. Without asking anybody's permission, that girl had gone off somewhere, with a boy, and they did not hear from her for years. In the family, they avoided talking about her and dodged any question to do with her. Only after Hanna grew up and started nagging her mother to tell her did she discover the little she knew about her aunt: Esther had learned to tailor the latest modes, she was very clever, very skilled, she had begun to earn quite good money, but instead of seeking a husband who would have been a 'good match' in the family's estimation – it would have been very easy for her to find a husband with a little capital, who would have opened a 'tailor's shop for ladies' for her in the centre of town – and instead of setting up home and having children, as her parents and brothers and sisters and grandparents and great-grandparents had, the girl took up with a young man, some kind of 'philosophy student,' an 'idealist,' one of those people who advocated a return to the ancestral places and occupations – the family didn't really know what that meant, they never got involved in politics of any kind – she went with him to some kind of camp, to learn how to 'work the land,' then after a few years they both went far away, to turn over the ancestral soil, to clear away the stones and yellow sand. It was not even known whether they had had a wedding, or even the semblance of a wedding, since they didn't invite anybody from the family. To the bewilderment and grief and annoyance of the Kamin family, a solid, respectable family of upstanding folk, in whose eyes that girl was insane, an adventuress. What was to be done? It would seem that in every good family, you could find a madcap like her.

The rag doll she received from Esta – the solemn-sounding 'Aunt Esther' didn't suit her at all – was very comical, hilarious even; it had a dress made of differently coloured cheap calico patches: red, blue, green, yellow, a pink hat sewn to its head, which meant it couldn't be taken off even at night when Hanna put it to bed, and on its white canvas face were traced in ink pencil two large dots: the eyes, a vertical line: the nose, and a horizontal line: the mouth. This small, scrawny, comical doll was dearer to Hanna than the other one. She loved it, cared for it, pampered it. The bed was just the right size for it, which meant the bedroom with the cupboard, little table, four chairs, everything belonged to the rag doll. Whereas the other doll, the chubby, blond doll with glassy blue eyes, had now become an ornament in the vitrine, alongside the porcelain crockery and some tarnished old silver trays and goblets. Once, her father brought her an expensive toy, a train with a black locomotive, a tender, an open freight car, and two passenger carriages, a train that ran around a track in a circle. Her mother scolded him: 'That's no toy for a little girl.' But Hanna liked it very much. She put a coat on the rag doll and placed it in the open freight car – it wouldn't fit through the doors of the passenger carriages – and let the train take the little girl for a ride, just has she had once gone on a train ride to the spa with her mother. It was so beautiful there in the countryside…

But most of all Hanna liked it in her father's watchmaker's shop. The shop was in the centre of town, or rather, not quite in the centre: turning aside from the busy, noisy main street, you went down a narrow, very quiet alley, where, apart from the watchmaker's shop, there was also a modest barber's shop with two chairs, where an old barber worked with an apprentice, who lathered the customers while they waited their turn to be shaved. It was there that her father went to get his hair cut or to have his round, chestnut-coloured beard trimmed when it grew too long. Outside, above the door of the watchmaker's shop, hung a tin sign, painted white and inscribed with blue letters: 'David Kamin, Watchmaker,' while inside, in the long, narrow room, there was an air of mystery. While her father sat leaning over a table covered with dismantled watches, springs, cogs, screws, with a black watchmaker's loupe over one eye, looking intently at the delicate mechanisms, trying to set in motion the stubborn cogs of some old Doxa pocket watch, the little girl would gaze in awe at all the wonders of that old shop. Indeed, when her father was not talking to a customer, a mysterious silence reigned in the watchmaker's shop. Clocks of every shape and size hung mutely on the walls. With their long metal pendulums capped with brass disks, or with their pinecone-shaped weights hanging from chains, all the clocks were designed for a strange purpose: The measurement of time. The measurement of that which does not exist, but which nonetheless elapses. It arrives, lingers for not even an instant, and imperceptibly passes, leaving deep traces…

Of all the large clocks, only one worked: a massive, stately horologe, housed in a rectangular box of black, ebony-like wood, with fortress turrets at the top, and whose enamelled face had elongated Roman numerals. It was by this clock that her father set his pocket watch, a thick, old silver Omega with a double lid, and by these two timepieces he would set the watches he repaired for his customers. 'It's ready,' her father would tell an impatient customer, 'but leave it with me for another twenty-four hours, to check how it keeps time.' The time kept by the watch had to match perfectly that kept by the clock on the wall with the elongated Roman numerals and by the Omega silver pocket watch.

David Kamin's watch repair business did not always do well; there were good times, when there was a lot of work, but there were also times of dearth. But while her parents fully felt the march of time and events, their little girl felt no great difference between the good times and the bad. She had everything she needed. It was the 1930s, when the market was flooded with those Japanese watches, dumped at cheap prices. The watch repairers were delighted at first. Everybody could now buy himself a watch, and more watches meant more repairs. But soon they realised they were completely wrong. Those Roskopf watches[6] were so cheap that it wasn't worth having them repaired; better to buy a new one. They were hard times for

---

6   Roskopf watches - Roskopf was a Swiss watchmaker who was one of the first to use stem-winding mechanisms to produce simple, robust, cheaply produced watches that were highly popular at the time

watch repairers, but they passed, like the hard times before them. And their daughter sensed nothing of it.

On Friday evenings, her mother would put on a white headscarf, wrap another around her daughter's head, and then light the Sabbath candles. She would cover her eyes with the palms of her hands and voicelessly moving her lips she would recite the prayer to Queen Sabbath. The little girl would watch in silence as her mother lit the candles, she would place her palms over her eyes and imitate the movements of her mother's lips.

On Sabbath afternoons, her father, his face rested, smooth – as if by miracle, not one wrinkle was visible, not one of the week's cares – would sit down at the table on the airy veranda and read from a thick old book bound in moth-eaten brown leather. More often than not he would sit his little girl on his knees and translate passages from the heavy tome for her. How dearly he would have liked to have had a boy. Which is to say, he would have liked to have a boy as well, who would have been able to recite, to learn the tiny letters… A little boy was to arrive two years after Hanna. But his wife Sara lost him in the sixth month, after which she became sickly and was unable to carry a pregnancy to term. He sent her to a spa – she went with their daughter Hanna, from whom she refused to be parted even for three weeks – important doctors examined her, it cost a fortune, only David Kamin and the Good Lord knew how hard it was. If only it had done any good, but it was all in vain. He thus had to resign himself and thank God above for his only child, who took the place of both a boy and a girl, of comfort and happiness, of everything in the life of the two parents.

Therefore, if the Lord had ordained there was not to be a son to learn how to read and interpret the tiny letters, then the task fell upon the daughter. At school, David Kamin's daughter learned reading and arithmetic, and later history and geography, natural science, physics, chemistry and many other humanist subjects, and a very good job too – he would let her learn as much as she was capable of learning, he would let her study for as many years as she wanted and maybe even take 'adult' classes – but it was imperative that a girl like Hanna Kamin also know a little about those old books, which told of the creation of the world and the first people, Adam and Eve, about how they were banished from Paradise, about the wretched Cain who out of envy slew his younger brother Abel, about the three patriarchs, Abraham, Isaac and Jacob, about the four matriarchs, Sara, Rebecca, Rachel and Leah, about how Jacob, tricked by his father-in-law Laban, was forced to work twice seven years for his two wives, about the great flood and Noah's Ark, thanks to which people and the beasts of the earth survived, about the sinful cities of Sodom and Gomorrah, about the exodus from the bondage of Mitzrayim… They were historical events… But what import, how many hidden meanings those events had! Every word had been weighed, every letter had been numbered by the sages of centuries past… How much of all this could the mind of a girl understand? His son might even have ventured among the tiniest of the letters, among the commentaries and glosses in the margins of the pages, which not even David Kamin had ever been able to understand… But even so, a girl like Hanna Kamin had to listen to the swaying verses of the Psalms of King David and the sentences of wise Solomon: 'Vanity of vanities, all is vanity! What profit hath a man of all his labour which he taketh under the sun?' Such words entered her ears almost without leaving a trace, but how lovely the verse of the Song of Songs sounded: 'Beautiful thou art, my love, beautiful thou art and there is no fault in thee… Thou hast ravished mine heart with the searching of thine eyes.' And her father would hasten to explain that it referred to the love between God Above and His people… Sometimes he would explain the meaning of the injunctions of the wise men: 'The men of the Great Assembly said: Be moderate and prudent, be not hasty to pronounce judgement… Jehoshua the son of Perahia said: Judge each man for the best… And the great scholar Hillel used to say: Be among the disciples of Aharon, love peace and pursue peace, love men and strive to bring them closer to the teaching… It was also he who said: Judge not your fellow man until you yourself have been in the same situation… Every love depends on a thing, and when the thing perishes, so does the love, but the love that depends not on a thing, never perishes.' And so, when she was little, every Sabbath afternoon, her father took her on his knees and read and translated to her passages from the thick old book bound in moth-eaten leather. Pointlessly, in fact, because the girl judged nobody and desired peace – she knew of war only from the history books – and loved everybody… But her father read to her, explained to her, melodiously murmured the verses, until the old man fell asleep with his head resting on the yellow pages of the book, whereupon the girl would tiptoe out of the glassed-in veranda, run to her room, to that comical rag doll with the white canvas face on which were drawn in ink pencil two dots: the eyes, a vertical line: the nose, a horizontal line: the mouth; or she would run outside to play with the other children. And later, when she was older, she would go for a walk with the girls from her class at school, in the overgrown park at the edge of town, where they would laugh and have fun reading the pink billets-doux that a freckled, lovestruck lycée boy sent to one of them in secret, a girl who, alas! was cold and lucid in the face of all his implorations… The envelopes were inscribed in a neat calligraphic hand, 'Strictly secret and personal, to the esteemed Miss…' and contained impassioned epistles such as this: 'Ever since I first saw you I have had no peace… You are the light of my eyes… At night, when the moon rises in the sky, I think of your dear face…' and so on.

Her mother, Riva Kamin, thin and small of frame as she was, but lively and industrious, little by little initiated her daughter into the secrets of housekeeping – 'a girl must know how to cook and to keep a clean house, no matter how much book-learning she acquires' – and in the evening, after work, she would sometimes have her sit down with her and read to her from the dog-eared book her own mother had inherited from her mother before her, whose mother had inherited it from her grandmother, and so on for nobody knows how many generations, a book that had the strange title *Tzeena Ureena*, which is to say, 'Let's go out and see!' A naïve, wonderful book that retold for the common reader, and the female reader in particular, wise parables and meaningful tales from other old books… Hanna clearly remembered one of those strange and terrible stories that her mother used to read to her, tears filling her eyes behind her wire-framed spectacles and in a sad, monotonous voice: it was the story of a city destroyed because of a cart pole. The king's daughter was passing through that city when the shaft of her carriage snapped. She commanded that a young fir tree planted at the birth of a child be cut down, at which the people of the city rebelled against their rulers. And there was another story about another city that was destroyed because of a hen and a cock, which the guests at a wedding were carrying at the head of a procession and which were stolen by foreign soldiers. And about another city that came to be razed because of the humiliation suffered by a man told to get up and leave the table at a feast, and not one of the other guests had protested or come to his defence… And so it was that in one part of the city there was merrymaking, while in the other the slaughter began. And those who made merry did not hear the cries of those hewn with swords and pierced with spears. In one part of the city, the wine flowed, in the other, blood…

To the girl's parents her path was clear. She would go to school for as long as she wanted, learn as much as her head could hold, take 'adult' classes, if she wanted. Why not? Then, with God's help, Hanna would get married, start a family, have children. Her parents, Riva and David Kamin, had even agreed on whom her husband would be… True, they had agreed by means of exchanged glances more than words. Jacob, Abramovitch's son. The Abramovitches had a hatter's workshop, you might even say a hat factory. A very good family. With the boy's father, Mr Efraim Abramovitch, they sat on adjacent thrones in the synagogue on the corner of the street; he was a distinguished man, well read, a good businessman. It was Abramovitch himself who had had the idea of starting a hat factory – not an overcoat or shirt or trouser factory, but a factory for hats, which can be made from leftover cloth – it was a very good idea and he seemed to be doing very well. The factory was expanding very nicely. He had started out with three sewing machines, he now had twelve, and tomorrow, who knows? Maybe a tall chimney would rise above the building… And their son Jacob, an only child, was clever; even now, he helped the old man run the factory. And the Kamins had a beautiful daughter with golden hair and blue eyes, a good, clever, well-behaved, obedient girl…

The children knew each other. They had grown up on the same street. Sometimes they met and talked. Jacob was not very interested in books, he had struggled to finish gymnasium school and then abandoned lycée, but on the other hand, he was passionate about hats. Wherever he saw an interesting hat, even if it was on somebody's head, a friend's or a stranger's, he would take it off or ask to see it, bashfully apologising, he would turn it on every side, examining the shape, the cloth, the stitching… With Hanna he was shy, but when he talked to her about hats he grew impassioned. He would tell her about the plans he was hatching in his mind, about how he was going to make a new design of hat, which would be good for both winter and summer, with a detachable lining and earflaps. He was also thinking of other hat designs, both stylish and practical.

Hanna had absolutely no interest in hats, but she listened to him in amusement. His shyness made her laugh. One day, Jacob spotted her in the street – she didn't know why, but she had the impression that he had been waiting for her – he went up to her and started to talk to her in a low, secretive voice:

'Hanna… there's something I'd like to tell you…'

'Then tell me, Jacob!' she replied, in surprise.

'You see, Hanna… I have… for a long time I have been thinking about you…' Jacob's face turned as red as a lobster and his tongue became even more tied. 'What I mean, Hanna… I have thought of something… to do with you, Hanna…'

Hanna remained silent, gazing at him curiously with her large, blue eyes. Jacob avoided her gaze and then plucking up the courage, quickly uttered his confession of love:

'I have been thinking of a hat design for girls, with a pompon in lots of different colours, which will be called the Hanna. The Hanna hat… It will sell like hot cakes. You'll see, Hanna… You'll see…'

Hanna was hard put not to burst out laughing.

So, her parents had thought it all out; her path was clearly laid out. The youngsters would be together, they would start a family, they would be upstanding, industrious people, with their own house, like their parents, their grandparents, their great-grandparents.

But how could those nice people, her parents, David Kamin and his wife Riva, have known that their daughter sooner resembled Aunt Esther, the 'Esta' who had once given her that comical rag doll? How could her parents have suspected that in her, in Hanna, there lurked a madcap, an adventuress like Esther?

Or even worse than Esther.

It had all happened with astonishing speed. Within a few months, one spring, one torrid summer, like in a film unreeling not in slow motion, so that you can see every single frame, or at normal speed, the same as in everyday life, but faster and faster, with everything happening before you have time to realise when and how it happened.

It was her final year of lycée, before the baccalaureate. Hanna had a classmate, Helena Bistricki, her best friend, and she used to go to her house to revise for the exams. They had so much coursework to study, but mathematics and chemistry in particular gave them a terrible headache. It was hard to absorb so many formulas and sums, but in the company of Helena, a clever, lively girl, studying seemed to go more easily.

It was here, at her friend's house, that she met Theodor, Helena's cousin on her father's side, who was in his final year at university. He was studying agronomy and had come to stay with his aunt and uncle, Helena's parents, to revise for his final exams, and also to spend the holiday. Theodor was tall and had sleek dark brown hair, which he wore in a perfect side-parting, dark eyes, a slightly hooked nose, and a protruding chin, which lent his face a manly expression. He talked to the girls in a superior, slightly ironical manner. He explained certain chemical formulas and complex calculations to them with bored, irritated politeness. 'This is the way to calculate it, mesdemoiselles!… Insert another hydrogen atom there, otherwise it will take you till the end of time to get the calculation right, mesdemoiselles!… You need a plus sign here, not a minus, mesdemoiselles!' He was obliging, but it was as if by his tone of voice he were saying, 'Come, come, you silly geese, don't gulp down the formulas whole without chewing them, use those silly little heads of yours to think about their separate ingredients! And then it will be easier for you to remember them!'

The girls regarded him with admiration, like an omnipotent deity of figures and formulas. But what surprised Hanna in particular was that Theodor also knew those thick old books from which her father read on Saturday afternoons. Once, in the evening, worn out by so much studying, the three of them were sitting on the couch, Helena, Hanna, and between them Theodor, when he began to quote from Solomon's Song of Songs: 'Beautiful thou art, my love, beautiful thou art, and I find no fault in thee… Thou hast stolen away my heart with the searching of thine eyes… How sweet are thy caresses, my sister, my bride…' But whereas in her father's mouth the words sounded ethereal, seraphic, like the love of Him Above for His people, in Theodor's mouth they sounded ironical, carnal, provocative. In the semi-darkness that had settled over the room, Hanna felt the blood rushing to her cheeks. And then, when he recited other verses, from the New Testament, which Hanna had never heard before, the words sounded very earthly: 'Let us hold fast the profession of our faith without wavering. And let us consider one another to provoke unto love and to good works.' Theodor had learned them by heart, long ago, in religious studies lessons, the subject in which he had had the best marks.

A few days later, Theodor Bistricki went back to university. In the midst of her exams, Helena received a letter from him. At the end, in a sort of post-scriptum, Theodor had added a few lines addressed to Hanna. It began, 'Dear Miss Hanna,' and continued with a few pieces of advice, offered half-seriously, half-ironically, to the effect that she should not be afraid, that she should not be flustered in front of the examiners, and that he, Theodor, had, thank God, taken numerous exams thitherto and had come to the conclusion that the panel of examiners were usually made up of teachers, and that teachers were human, too… And he ended the letter by wishing her the best of success.

Hanna asked her friend to send him her warmest greetings and best wishes for success in his exams when she replied to his letter. To which Theodor replied straight away, writing inconsequential pleasantries to his cousin, teasing her the same as ever, but appending a separate note for Hanna. This time, the note began, 'Esteemed Miss Hanna,' and continued in the same ironical tone, saying that even a person up to her ears in revising for exams might still make the effort to pen a few lines to him in her own little hand… Hanna replied, penning a few lines at the end of her friend's letter. She tore up four or five drafts; she didn't know how to begin, how to conclude, what to write in the middle. In the end, Helena dictated most of it to her… But for a fact, it was written in 'her own little hand.' To which she received a reply in an elegant envelope bearing Theodor's elegant seal, slipped inside the larger envelope containing the inconsequential, teasing letter to his cousin Helena…

That same summer holiday, after the girls passed their baccalaureate – by a whisker, as they say: in mathematics and chemistry they were on the verge of drowning and barely reached the other bank, clinging to a straw – and after Theodor received his diploma in agronomic engineering, cum maxima laude, he came to visit his aunt, uncle and cousin Helena once more, for another holiday. This time, he didn't have the worry of revision, exams, dissertations and colloquia. The three youngsters, Helena, Theodor and Hanna, were to be seen together more and more often, in town, at the cake shop, in the park; they took long walks together and excursions to the surrounding countryside, they talked and laughed together. After which, just the two of them were to be seen together, Hanna and Theodor. They felt happy when they were with each other and gradually they began to feel unhappy when they were not with each other. The town, which was small and full of gossips, began to talk. Some of which talk also reached the ears of her parents, who began to have words with the girl, at first gently and indirectly, but then more and more angrily. What was the point? He wasn't her type, they weren't suited to each other and they never would be… She needed to realise who she was and who he was… To open her eyes and ears and mind. Her father ended up shouting at her, something he had never done before. And her mother, in the evenings after work, would lay aside that book, *Tzeena Ureena*, which it was obvious she did not have the strength to read, she would have her sit beside her and talk to her in a voice that was full of pain:

'Hanna, what are you doing? Don't you think of us? Is this what we deserve from you, your mother and father?'

Hanna kept her silence. She could not understand what she was doing wrong by going for walks with Theo, who was an intelligent and cultured young man, a courteous and handsome young man, such as a girl rarely has a chance to meet. But what did her parents know? They were simple folk, good, modest, wrapped up in their own world… Hanna would keep an annoyed silence until she could no longer bear to listen to them and then she would burst into tears and run to her room.

When she told Theodor what was happening to her at home, the young man burst out laughing. Exactly the same thing was happening to him. His parents had written to him to come home. They said that there was no point in him staying so long in that town, at his uncle's, when his parents were waiting for him and there were so many things to be done at home. His uncle and aunt were nagging him, too. Lucky that Helena took his side and shouted at her parents: 'What do you know? You see a girl go for a walk with a boy two or three times and jump to who knows what conclusion!' Theodor's parents lived in the countryside, where they had land, a small manor house, and a liqueur factory. 'North-East' cherry liqueur was highly prized by connoisseurs. That was what his parents excelled at, Theodor told the girl, they were good businessmen, hard-working, his father and mother worked from dawn to dusk, supervising the servants and farmhands, taking care of business. But they had numerous prejudices. People of the last century… 'Theo, don't go out with that girl, she's poor!' 'Don't go out with that other girl, she's not of our faith!' 'Don't go out with that one, she's not of our race!'…

'And here I am, with all of those faults: I'm not of the same race, I'm not of the same faith, and I'm poor to boot! A fine choice you made, Theo!' laughed Hanna.

'Didn't I tell you, they're old-fashioned and full of prejudices?'

In the midst of the increasingly exasperating din of backbiting, gossip and whispers, the young couple had a refuge, a place of their own, a place for nobody but them, an oasis of peace and quiet. It was next to the River Domolu, as that sluggish yellow stream that flowed at the edge of town was called. Along the riverbank there were wide expanses of maize. Theodor had beaten a hidden path there, which led to a small clearing in the maize field. There they lay in each other's arms looking up at the blue sky, all alone with their love, with the depths of the sky above them, across which sailed translucent white clouds, making it seem even deeper and bluer, all alone within the dense maize and sunflower stalks, through which slipped only the pure whisper of the faint, caressing breeze and the scent of plants that took honest joy in the light, the air, the sap of the earth… Other people's whispers could not reach them there. There they felt without sin and without blemish. There they were truly happy…

The situation was becoming tenser and tenser, the letters from his father more and more categorical, and Theodor detected in them more and more vigorous statements on the part of his mother, whom he could almost see standing behind her husband, watching every letter, every word that issued from his pen. 'It's all because of you, all because you were too soft on him that he's turned out so impertinent and disobedient!'

His father wrote that he must come home immediately, and the word 'immediately' was underlined three times in desperation. His parents went so far as to write to his uncle and aunt, Helena's parents, demanding they send him home immediately. Again, 'immediately' was underlined three times. That they should not keep him in their house a moment longer, in other words, that they quite simply turf him out. It was more than certain that his aunt and uncle had better things to do than write to his parents about every time he met with Hanna. His father, old man Marian Bistricki, had hardly been able to wait for his only son to finish university and obtain his diploma in agronomic engineering. He had big plans for him, he wanted him to look after his hectares of land and start producing new types of liqueur distilled from medicinal herbs – he had even thought of a brand name for them: 'Liqueur of Life.' Elderflower liqueur, linden liqueur, peppermint liqueur, centaury liqueur… But for that, what was required was the devotion, drive, and education of the son of whom he was so proud.

'Yes, the old man has big plans,' said Theodor, in a voice in which irony mingled with compassion. 'But what can I do to help him?'

Theodor did not wish to embark on life leaning on crutches placed under his arms by his father. He wanted to go off somewhere and make a fortune by his own hard work. And his mother, the distinguished Lady Marilena Bistricki, a woman of noble stock, full of energy and ambition – it was from her that his father had the land and the manor house where he had built his liqueur factory – was surely waiting for him at home with a good match, a girl of good family, with a big dowry, a very big dowry… Who knows what spoiled, insensate young lady she had picked, somebody with whom you could neither talk nor sit in silence: there you are, Theodor, live your whole life with her, be happy! Love? They had long ago forgotten the meaning of the word, if they had ever known it…

'Our poor parents, I don't condemn them, God forbid, but they are so old-fashioned and riddled with prejudices and superstition! Both mine and yours, Hanna!' said Theodor, with finality.

Indeed, in the Kamin household, the situation was by no means any better. Nor did it improve with the passage of time. All day long, Riva, the girl's mother, went around like a silent ghost, with tearful eyes, heaving deep sighs, or else talking in a faint, weary voice, she wandered from room to room, murmuring prayers known to her alone, in the kitchen she would quench burning coals in a glass of water, reciting charms against the evil eye, and her father, gentle, brown-haired watchmaker David Kamin, who would not have harmed a fly, thought more and more often of sending her away from home, as far away as possible, to stay with a relative or in a strict boarding house for girls, where she would learn the proper respect and obedience due to her parents! Yes, he wanted to send her away, their only child, Hanna, from whom they had not been parted a single day. Or else overcome by fits of rage, David Kamin would decide for the umpteenth time quite simply to shut her in the damp, dark cellar, to place a heavy padlock on the door, not to let the girl see the light of day until she returned to her senses…

That was how things stood when the tragedy occurred, which shook the town, rousing it from the sticky torpor of that summer. At the dawn of a market day, a few peasants from the surrounding countryside were making their way to town along the bank of the Domolu when they espied the cap of a uniform bobbing on top of the maize, rolling back and forth in the wind. As it struck them as odd, quite rightly so, they went to have a closer look. In a little clearing among the tall maize stalks, they found the lifeless bodies of two young people in an embrace: an officer in uniform and a girl in a flowery silk dress. Both had been shot in the heart with the revolver still clenched in the officer's right hand, and they lay in a pool of blood. The investigation quickly and easily established the facts, identified the bodies, and reconstructed exactly what had happened. With sensational headlines and entire columns of newsprint, the local paper described the tragedy in copious detail. The young couple were Miriam, the most beautiful girl in town, a brunette with dark eyes, the daughter of a well-known silk merchant, and a young officer, the most handsome, most able, and most dashing lieutenant in the garrison. Three days previously, a hot, sunny Sunday, she had put on her most beautiful, flowery dress, and he had put on his dress uniform. They had met in their usual spot, on the riverbank, they had then gone into the maize field, he had hung his cap on a tall stalk, to mark the spot so they could be found, they had lain down next to each other, in an embrace, he had fired a bullet in her heart and then shot himself in the heart. That was how they were found three days later, their young bodies beginning to decay. In the pocket of the lieutenant's uniform had been found a note signed by both of them, in which they begged their parents' forgiveness, they knew what grief they would suffer, but they had had no choice, and they begged that they at least be buried together, if it had not been fated that they should live together. But what had not been possible so long as they were alive, that is, to be parted, was perfectly possible after their death. They were buried separately, he in a Christian cemetery, she in a Jewish cemetery. It could not have been otherwise, since she had not been baptised and he had not converted to Judaism.

The town was shaken. Parents shed copious, heavy tears over the long columns of newsprint, the fathers and mothers of marriageable girls cited the case as an example, a deterrent: 'See what happened if they didn't obey their parents!' Young people, thrilled by the towering love and courageous act of the officer and the girl, who committed suicide by revolver, like in a novel, procured photographs of them from a photographer in town. The photographer, a canny and enterprising man, who had separate clichés of the pair, made a montage of the two lovers, in which they were together, smiling, happy and serene… The boys carried this photograph in their breast pockets, the girls pasted it in their scrapbooks…

The town was in an uproar. For weeks, people commented, argued, condemned, defended. Look at where prejudices and superstitions lead! They shouldn't have disobeyed their parents! Their parents should never have let things go so far! But what could they have done? What do you mean, what? They should have demanded the lieutenant be transferred to a different garrison, somewhere far away, at the other end of the country. And her parents should have sent her to a different town, to stay with relatives, they should have locked her in the house, or even in the cellar, with a padlock on the door, so that she wouldn't go roaming wherever the fancy took her… Who has ever heard of a girl from a decent family having assignations with a young man in a cornfield?…

Now that the tragedy had occurred, everybody was wise after the fact, they all knew what the parents ought to have done and what they ought not to have done, and what they would have done in their place…

Most shaken of all at what had happened were Hanna and Theodor. They looked at each other, turning white. It was like an omen to them. The tragedy had taken place on the bank of the River

Domolu, in the very same cornfield, near the spot where they themselves took refuge, their 'oasis of happiness'…

'Do you know what I would like to do now, Hanna? I would like to go to their parents and ask them which they preferred: two children dead in a cornfield, but apart, or two living children, who lived happily together? What do you think they would answer?'

Yes, they had to leave that town as quickly as possible. Theodor would find a job on a farm somewhere, in some village where nobody knew him. Their parents would be furious, so much he knew. They would disinherit him; that was the classic recourse. But what else could they do? Hanna's parents would disown her, their daughter, too. They would both write to their parents and ask them to understand. To forgive them. There was nothing else they could do. And in time, her parents and his would grow used to it and forgive them…

They made the decision one evening, sitting on a bench in the park. Since the 'tragedy' they had stopped going to that place of theirs by the River Domolu. Hanna could no longer control herself and burst into tears. A fit of tears. The tragedy of the young couple in the cornfield, their own situation, the decision to leave her parents' house in secret: far too many things had accumulated…

And it turned out the way they had suspected rather than the way they had hoped. Their parents did not understand. Neither his nor hers… Riva, that frail woman, who spent every day busy in the kitchen and lit the Sabbath candles every Friday evening and read *Tzeena Ureena*, understood nothing. Nor did David Kamin, who spent the whole week repairing people's watches and setting their time by the big wall clock with Roman numerals and by his old silver Omega, and who on Sabbath afternoons read from that thick, old, moth-eaten book, did not understand. Those two people understood nothing. What had happened? That blow, long foreboded, was nonetheless so unexpected. What had happened to their daughter, such a good and obedient girl?… She had died. To them, it was as if she were dead. Their only child had died, who had sat on their knees and learned the wisdom of their ancestors, the child who had taken the place of both a boy and a girl, who had given them comfort hope, everything. In fact, it was worse than death. If she had died, they would have wept and moaned at her bedside, they would have rent their clothes, and they would have known she was buried in a corner of the Jewish cemetery, where other young girls like her rested, and they would have been able to say like sorely afflicted Job: 'The Lord giveth, the Lord taketh away, blessed be the name of the Lord'… But as it was, who had taken their daughter away? What was certain was that her parents understood nothing. They paced back and forth in bewilderment all day long, uncomprehending. They were ashamed. Riva was ashamed to leave the house. Her father was ashamed to go to the synagogue, to sit on his chair on the eastern wall, opposite the curtain of the holy ark, sewn with gold thread, he was ashamed before Abramovitch, whose chair was next to his, before Abramovitch's son, before the whole congregation of that synagogue of which he was a founding member. David Kamin's hair turned completely white in the space of a few days, and Hanna's mother became smaller, more withered.

From far away, from the village where her husband had got a job as an agronomic engineer on a farm and where it was now a cold autumn of wind and rain and yellowed leaves falling from the trees in front of her window, Hanna wrote to her parents. The letter was brief, its sentences interrupted by febrile weeping… 'Forgive me, dear parents, I know it is hard for you, but try to understand me. I couldn't do otherwise, just as Theodor couldn't do otherwise… Please forgive me! Please… Please… Maybe the day will come when you will be able to regard us both, Theodor and me, as your children. Despite every prejudice, we remain your children… Father, you taught me our ancestors' words of wisdom… "Be prudent, do not be hasty to pronounce judgement… Do not judge your neighbour until you have been in the same situation as him." Forgive me Mama, Mammy! Forgive me, Daddy!'

She was never to find out whether or not her parents forgave her.

As they waited for a letter, for good news or even the slightest sign of reconciliation and forgiveness on the part of their parents – they knew that in the end it would have to arrive – the young couple's life in the country, that autumn, was quite amusing at first. Everything was new to them: the places, the people, and then came a long, white, monotonous winter, followed by that hot, unforgiving spring…

The village was quite well off, the centre of an administrative district, surrounded by other smaller villages and hamlets, which stretched along the valleys and over the hills round about. The village lay along both sides of a main road, which formed the high street. The high street intersected with smaller lanes, each with its own name. Or rather its nickname, since none of the lanes had official name plaques, and all the houses in the village were numbered from one to one thousand three hundred and something. But from the most distant times, the villagers had given each lane its own picturesque nickname: Ram's Lane, Nanny-goat Lane, Cherry Tree Lane, Appletree Lane, Walnut Tree Lane, Spring Lane, Cuckoo Lane. Nobody knew where the name Cuckoo Lane had come from, since cuckoos could be heard singing on every lane in the village, and likewise cherry, apple and walnut trees grew in every orchard there, rams and nanny-goats could be found in almost every yard, and spring came to the whole village when it was time to come.

The village had a church, a synagogue, a primary school, two taverns, three general stores, a shop for cloth and fabrics, a pharmacy. At the edge of the village, in the middle of a thick pine forest, there was a sanatorium for tuberculosis patients.

The church stood on a small hill on Main Street and had a tall spire capped with a gilded cross, and within the belfry there were three brass bells, each with a different chime. The synagogue was also on the main road, at the intersection with Walnut Tree Lane, also known as Jews' Lane, although Jews also lived on other lanes in the village. The two taverns grandly styled themselves a 'buffet' and a 'restaurant.' They were not content merely with the grand names, but also had brightly coloured signboards, whose crooked red, green and blue letters proclaimed in the proprietors' idiosyncratic spelling: 'Buffetu-Elite' and 'Restorantu Splendide.' The reason for these names was unknown, since both taverns sold liquor that was equally strong and food that was equally poor, and the floors of both establishments were equally dotted with drunkards' globs of phlegm. The cloth store kept all kinds of textiles, fabrics and small items, all of them cheap, since there was no point in stocking more expensive goods: villagers who desired good-quality cloth or real silk went into town, where they had a better choice. The pharmacy had a serious-looking sign above the door, with the words 'Farmacia Hypocrates' inscribed in silver letters on a black background, and on both sides of the entrance were oval shields of black metal, each with a silver snake coiled around a mortar of the same colour: the emblem of the guild. The 'Hypocrates' sign and the two shields undoubtedly wakened fear and respect in the villagers. The three general stores competed with each other fiercely, and besides the usual 'colonial wares and delicacies' also stocked a host of household items, ranging from darning needles to machines for mincing cattle fodder, from illustrated postcards, wedding, baptism and holiday greetings cards, and black-edged paper for letters of condolence to gum Arabic, toilet paper, and ingenious mousetraps and rat poison, depending on how the esteemed customer wished to exterminate his rodents. The customer came first! One of the proprietors, a lively, enterprising man, had once even come up with the brilliant idea of selling powdered aspirin, which, because of people's frequent headaches, had become a bestselling item. The other two general stores, which were not to be outdone, were on the verge of copying the same idea, when a conflict broke out with the proprietor of the 'Hypocrates' pharmacy, Mr Edvard Maturinski, who went to court. Mr Maturinski objected that aspirin was plainly a medicament and consequently could be sold only in pharmacies, to which Mr Mendel Rubinhertz, the lively, enterprising general store proprietor, rejoindered that bicarbonate of soda was a medicament for the stomach, that honey was sometimes a medicament, too, that rusks and biscuits and corn oil and other foodstuffs were medicaments for patients on a diet. Unsurprisingly, Mr Rubinhertz lost the court case. Every judge, from the district court to the appeals court, ruled that while honey and bicarbonate and rusks may in certain circumstances be medicaments, aspirin was never, under any circumstance, a foodstuff…

The farm at which agronomic engineer Theodor Bistricki worked was not large, but the work was interesting and varied. The farm had cereal crops and a cherry orchard, in a valley sheltered from the region's cold winds. It also had a herd of thoroughbred cows and a small milk processing facility that made cream, cheese and butter. Engineer Bistricki was kept very busy and soon came to realise that book-learning was one thing and everyday practical work quite another. Hanna was busy with domestic affairs, with cleaning, cooking, washing, and she too realised, more than once, that it was one thing to have seen her mother performing such tasks, and to have helped her when she had the time and patience, and quite another to do them herself, since otherwise they would never have got done.

The owners of the farm never showed themselves in the village. They had other farms and lived in the capital and abroad. The farm was run by an administrator, Mr Pattunek, a man almost two metres tall, with a broad back, sturdy and taciturn. He gave curt orders and advice. At the end of every month, after the books were balanced and the wages paid, Mr and Mrs Bistricki were invited to have tea with Mr and Mrs Pattunek. The administrator's wife was a very beautiful, very distinguished woman. She wore her black hair in a plait coiled around her head like a crown. Her large, dark, sad eyes seemed to conceal some impenetrable mystery. She looked much younger than her husband, but she was just as taciturn and shut up within herself as he was. People could not understand how a woman such as she could live so secluded a life.

All the village notables were invited to these tea parties: Mr Andruschka the notary public and his wife; Dr Halinski the director of the tuberculosis hospital and his wife; Mr Maturinski the pharmacist; Father Ignatius, who drank only tea with a thin slice of lemon, never laced with rum or other alcoholic beverages; Mr Galagonitch, the headmaster of the primary school, a timid man, tall, thin, blond, who would always retire to the same corner of the salon with his cup of tea, from whence he would smile shyly at the rest of the company. Although he was married, he came without his wife, who had to stay at home with the children – theirs was an impoverished household, with one child in each of the four forms of the primary school, one in nursery school, and one in the cradle. At these monthly gatherings, little was said, little was drunk, and the silence was great. Besides, administrator Pattunek's reception room was too large and too sumptuous – the walls were painted a dark green, with gold leaf in the corners, and walnut wainscots – for you to feel at ease, for you to talk freely, and you would therefore end up making only hushed remarks at intervals, about the weather, about the clouds that threatened rain, about the political clouds that threatened a storm and which smelled of gunpowder, as Andruschka the notary public would self-importantly opine.

By contrast, at the Sunday-evening tea parties held by rotation at the notary's, the doctor's, the pharmacist's, and, since his arrival in the village, the agronomic engineer's, the talk was far noisier. They would drink and converse about all kinds of things; they would play all kinds of card games: rummy, poker, sixty-six, eight-nine, to make it more varied.

Mr Thaddeus Andruschka, the notary, was the most enthusiastic of the company and usually arrived first, arm in arm with his wife. Mr Andruschka was a man in his fifties, short, bald to his nape, with just two tufts of ginger hair above his ears. He had dark rings under his small, lively eyes. He walked with a thick, steel-tipped oak cane, so as not to slip, since he had a wooden leg, having lost a limb during the 1914–18 war. He had fought at Doberdo and Plave, and in exchange for his leg, he had received a wooden one and a decoration for bravery, of which he was very proud. Mrs Elvira Andruschka was a tall woman, as skinny as a plank, with a wrinkled face and curls of chestnut hair plastered over her forehead. She appeared to have been beautiful once. She never contradicted her husband, whose intelligence she seemed to admire deeply. She agreed unreservedly with everything the notary said and opened her mouth only after looking in her husband's eyes and divining therein whether she had permission to offer an opinion or not.

After Mr and Mrs Andruschka, Mr Maturinski the pharmacist would be the next to arrive for Sunday tea. Mr Edvard Maturinski also walked with a cane, but without needing to. His was a slender, elegant cane with a silver handle, which perfectly suited his elegant attire, which looked like it was fresh out of the box. He always dressed in black, with a white shirt and impeccable necktie. He was tall, his manly face was pockmarked, black, bushy eyebrows framed his green eyes, and he wore his dark hair slicked back, with a perfect centre parting. He would kiss Hanna's hand and shake her husband's with the urbanity of a man of the world. He was a bachelor, the village gallant, rumoured to have had numerous affairs, although nothing was known for sure.

After him, Mr and Mrs Halinski would arrive. Dr Andrei Halinski, the director of the local tuberculosis hospital, was a small, swarthy, quarrelsome man. He was very solemn, but his solemnity quickly dissolved after the first glass of brandy, whereupon he would become merry, exuberant, raucous, he would laugh loudly and sometimes without reason, causing his wife, who set great store by good manners, to attempt to quell him, casting apologetic glances all around. Mrs Magdalena Halinski was a sturdy, voluminous woman, with brawny arms and legs – in his youth the doctor had fallen in love with the well-built nurse and taken her for his wife without a second thought, despite his family's objections. Her blond hair contrasted strongly with her small, round, child-like face.

Although all the guests at these Sunday afternoons and evenings were older than they were, Hanna and Theodor Bistricki found entertainment in their company. They played cards and drank tea laced with rum, copious rum, and as time wore on, even neat rum without the tea, or brandy, with sweet liqueurs for the ladies, and they conversed on every possible subject, combining every possible topic. The women would talk about fashions, about silk stockings, about how expensive they were and how quickly they tore, about how impertinent the servants were becoming nowadays, while the men would make philosophical observations about politics, about women, about life in general, and sometimes about the Jews. It was an increasingly fashionable topic.

'Whoever it was who said it had a point when he said that they're like salt in food. If there's too much salt, the food's no good… *Pas parole!*' said Mr Andruschka, his face red after one glass of tea and three of rum. 'In the past, they weren't allowed to settle in the countryside. After which, they lived on just a single lane. But now they're everywhere. Wherever you go, like it or not, you trip over them…'

His wife Elvira nodded her curl-plastered forehead and looked around her radiantly, waiting for these wise words to take their effect on the other guests.

Hanna felt the blood rushing to her cheeks.

'But what have they ever done to you, Mr Andruschka?' she asked in a choked voice, trembling with annoyance.

'What have they done? What have they done? They've made him rich!' Mr Maturinski the pharmacist instantly replied on behalf of the notary, whom the hostess's question had taken by surprise.

'Yes, they've made him rich!' said Dr Halinski and burst out laughing. 'You're right there! They've made him rich! Ha, ha, ha!'

Mrs Halinski pinched his arm and whispered to him in embarrassment, 'Don't laugh so loudly, Andrei, it's not the done thing…'

But the doctor's laughter was infectious and the others started laughing too.

It was true: at the time, the Jews had to obtain all kinds of official documents, certificates and attestations. A series of laws, decrees and ordinances required them to prove even the most obvious things. They had to obtain stamped and signed official papers to prove that they had been born, where and when they had been born, where they were domiciled and since when, that they were Jewish, that they were citizens, that their parents had been born, had been domiciled, had been citizens, that their grandparents and great-grandparents had been born, had been domiciled, had been citizens. Then they had to prove that they had not been in trouble with the law, that they had been well behaved – a separate proof was required for this – that they were not behind with their taxes, and so on. And then all day, every day, they had to go to the mayor's office to pay fiscal stamps and notary fees and typed-copy fees and outstanding imposts. Outstanding imposts were always being found, to which accrued late-payment interest and fines…

'I don't want the notary coming to our house ever again! And I'm never going to his house again!' yelled Hanna after the guests had left.

Theodor burst out laughing and said, 'Did you really take him seriously, Hanna? Can't you see that the notary is just a salon anti-Semite? It's the done thing for an 'intellectual' to speak of the Jews like that… It's the current trend! On the other hand, it seems he helps them wherever he can…'

Father Ignatius, the village priest, also used to come to the Sunday-afternoon tea parties sometimes, but he never stayed very long, because he didn't want to make people feel uncomfortable by his presence. He drank tea only with a thin slice of lemon. He didn't take his tea laced with rum, he didn't drink brandy or any other alcoholic beverage, he didn't drink, he didn't play cards, and he never spoke of politics, women, or the Jews. He would come on Sunday afternoons only because he didn't want to bother people during the week, when he knew they were busy, and he knew that on that day of rest he would find them gathered together and would have an opportunity to speak to them about his church work, about his projects, about his collections for the needy before the holidays, or else sometimes he would make tactful, gentle allusion to the fact that some Christians neglected the holy sacrament of confession…

After the priest left, the notary would ironically remark, 'That man of God takes his work too seriously,' at which his wife would scold him, saying, 'How can you talk like that, Thaddeus, my dear!' It was the only subject on which Mrs Elvira Andruschka, who had been educated in a convent, did not wholeheartedly agree with her husband or nod her curl-plastered forehead.

Hanna, on the other hand, felt somehow singled out by the priest's allusions. She went to church every Sunday, as was the local custom, but she never went to confession. Even though Theodor, without insisting overly much, had advised her to do so, every now and then, at least for the sake of appearances… But she was afraid to. It was as if she would have had to get undressed in front of the priest, in that alcove of the church. She was embarrassed even to get undressed in front of the doctor, or as a matter of fact, even more so in a doctor's surgery. The priest was young and the church filled her with fear, she felt alien and out of place beneath the cold, lofty, solemn vaulted ceiling, even though she liked the priest's warm voice; it soothed her. Above all, she liked the sermons he gave from the high pulpit. His words sounded familiar and if she closed her eyes, they were like an echo from far away… Father Ignatius, for all his asceticism, was still a young man, he was in his forties, tall, slim, with swept-back chestnut hair, a strongly featured face, a slightly hooked nose, and deep, dark, piercing eyes, which sometimes blinked wearily, after so much searching for the truth in those numerous, closely-printed, small-lettered books with their cross references to so many other tomes.

Hanna listened to his deeply meaningful sermons, delivered in a warm, uplifting voice, she listened to him submissively and in her mind, she made the connection with other books that had once been read to her, when she was little and sat on her father's knees, or on a little stool next to her mother's apron, listening to the sad, monotonous murmur of her voice. Hanna was living a strange, double life. But even so, now that her two lives had coalesced, that one life became increasingly ordinary as the weeks passed, until it came to seem something normal. Nor could it have been otherwise. Every Friday evening, she put on her white headscarf, which was one of the few things she had taken with her from home, and she lit the two candles to greet the Sabbath. She lit the candles, covered her eyes with her palms, and prayed voicelessly, moving her lips, she prayed for her parents, for the souls of her grandparents and ancestors, and she would stand for a long while, sunk in formless, shapeless thoughts. Once, Theodor caught her standing like that, lost in thought in front of the lit candles, and gently scolded her: 'What are you doing, woman? You left the door open. Anybody could have come in. Somebody might have seen you and spread it all over the village. What good would it do complicating your life?' After that, Hanna lit the candles in the larder, among the bottles and jars; the larder had no windows, only a small, square aperture in the ceiling, which gave onto the attic. She would light small candles in there, on a silver tray, or rather candle stumps, so that they would burn down more quickly. She would stand before them with her hands over her eyes, until they burnt away, sometimes even long after they had gone out in the hidden darkness of the larder. And on Sunday morning, she would go to the village church and listen to the sermon of Father Ignatius. The priest spoke beautifully and what he said was mysterious and limpid at the same time. It always seemed to Hanna that what he said had a meaning beyond the words themselves, a meaning that she was unable to decipher. She had the feeling that his fervent words were addressed to her alone, that the priest knew everything about her, although she realised that he could not know anything, that he had no means of knowing, that he had never heard her confession and she had never told him anything, nor had Father Ignatius ever sought to glean from her anything more than she told him…

The priest's voice resounded from the pulpit, now gentle, now threatening, filling the stony hollow of the church:

'Fear has consumed us… Today, many have come to conceal their pure thoughts, thereby becoming strangers among their own… Parents who feel they must conceal themselves from their children, whom they conceived… Brothers forced by brothers to be parted in thought and in mind and in deed… Wherefore it is meet that we cry out in the words of St John: "Little children, it is the last time, and as ye have heard that antichrist shall come, even now are there many antichrists, whereby we know that it is the last time. They went out from us, but they were not of us… He is antichrist that denieth the Father and the Son. Whosoever denieth the Son, the same hath not the Father." Wherefore the wonderful exhortations of St Paul the Apostle are welcome in this present day: "Let brotherly love continue. Be not forgetful to entertain strangers, for thereby some have entertained angels unawares." And as the Old Testament tells us of the Patriarch Abraham, in the Book of Genesis, "And he lifted up his eyes and looked, and, lo, three men stood by him, and when he saw them, he ran to meet them from the tent door, and bowed himself toward the ground, and said, My Lord, if now I have found favour in thy sight, pass not away, I pray thee, from thy servant: Let a little water, I pray you, be fetched, and wash your feet, and rest yourselves under the tree: And I will fetch a morsel of bread, and comfort ye your hearts, after that ye shall pass on, for therefore are ye come to your servant. And they said, 'So do, as thou hast said.'"'

Hanna sat in her pew, motionless, she listened and was unable to decipher the hidden meaning of the words. But she had the feeling that it was about her and that the priest was addressing only her, and that he was looking at her from up there in the pulpit, with his dark, piercing eyes, which sometimes blinked, weary from the labour of the tiny letters…

She had no way of knowing that the others in church each had the same feeling too.

Of all her new acquaintances in the village, Hanna best liked Angela the midwife. Although her house on Ram's Lane had a plaque that said 'Qualified Midwife,' inscribed in large red letters, you never found her at home. She was like quicksilver, that woman of almost sixty, with very curly straw-yellow hair, which stubbornly poked from under her dark brown headscarf, with her green eyes and her long, pointy nose. She knew every woman in the commune and in the surrounding villages and hamlets, how her pregnancy was progressing, in what month she was, so that at the birth she would always appear in the evening without being called, without the poor husband having to pull on his trousers and run to fetch her in the middle of the night.

Angela had become very dear to Hanna. She might turn up at her house on any day of the week, at any time of day, morning, afternoon or evening, the time didn't matter, and she would go to Hanna wherever she was. If Hanna was in the kitchen, Angela would rummage through the drawers of the sideboard, make herself a cup of coffee or tea, sit down on a stool, ask her questions, and then start to tell her stories. Even though there was nobody else in the kitchen, in a hushed, secretive voice she would first of all ask whether there had been any signs… She would give advice to the young wife. And then she would start telling her stories. She knew everything that went on in the village and the surrounding hamlets, every event great and small, all the gossip, although she never believed the talk if it spoke ill of anybody. It was from Angela that Hanna discovered all the things people said about Edvard Maturinski the pharmacist, the village gallant, about how long ago he had had rather intimate relations with Elvira, the wife of Andruschka the notary, about how Elvira's eldest daughter, or her youngest son, bore a resemblance to Maturinski, although Angela herself could not see it, not one little bit… Mr Maturinski was also supposed to have had a romantic involvement with – 'whom do you think, Hanna? You'll never guess, of that I'm sure!' – Mrs Pattunek, Mrs Clara Pattunek, the overseer's wife, that beautiful woman with the mysterious eyes, who was said to be the daughter of down-at-heel nobles and hadn't for the life of her wanted to marry Mr Pattunek, a man who had made a fortune administering other people's estates… But Angela didn't believe it… The qualified midwife told stories about everybody and everything, but she never thought ill of anybody. Nor did she draw any distinction among people, labelling one person this and another that, commenting on how one person had such and such while another went without, observing that one person was big and another small… She knew from her extremely vast experience that every mother suffers the same throes of childbirth and that every person is born of a mother…

It was from Angela that Hanna first heard of Sara-Lea Berkowitz, a woman whom she was to see at close hand sooner than she would have imagined and in a circumstance so terrible. According to the qualified midwife, Sara-Lea Berkowitz lived in a dilapidated little cottage at the end of Walnut Tree Lane, also known as 'Jews' Lane,' she had four children and was expecting a fifth. She was in her fourth month, but the midwife was certain she was in her sixth… Her husband, Chaim Berkowitz, a poor tailor, otherwise a quiet and very hardworking man, who sewed and darned all day long, had fallen ill and they had admitted him to the tuberculosis sanatorium. And now Sara-Lea had to work single-handed to feed so many mouths. She also had to work to support her husband, who was no longer able to help her in any way. She had to buy bread, clothes and shoes for the children, firewood for heating and cooking, oil for the lamp… What could the poor woman do? She did the best she could, but even a fish out of water would have been in a better way than she… She took in laundry, she went to people's houses to do the cleaning. 'If only you could see the children, Hanna! The eldest, a lad of about eight, is in his second year at school and he writes so beautifully, his letters are like pearls, no less, and he can draw and do sums. He has a brain, the lad does, and no joke. And the little girl of six does the housework, you'd have to see it to believe it, Mrs Hanna Bistricki: the broom is twice as tall as her, but the little girl handles it like a grown up. And she also takes care of her two little brothers, when their mama isn't at home. The woman doesn't ask for any handouts from anybody. She washes laundry, she scrubs floors, she cleans windows, and she doesn't utter a word of complaint. Four mouths to feed, five if you count hers, and every now and then a bottle of milk to take to her husband in the hospital…' Angela alone knew what went on in that house. But she didn't go around telling everybody. She told only some people… And some people helped the woman out in what little ways they could…

Hanna searched through her cupboards and drawers, she found an old shirt of her husband's, which was still decent, and a dark brown sweater that Theodor had long since stopped wearing, she wrapped them up and gave them to Angela. She also gave her a few coins from her housekeeping money. To give that poor woman. But don't let Angela tell anybody…

It was also from Angela the qualified midwife that Hanna found out about the new official order, which had by then arrived in the village. The war was of course a topic of discussion at overseer Pattunek's monthly salon and the Sunday-afternoon card games that were held by rotation in the homes of the district's notables, but it seemed very far away. Young people had been conscripted from the village, telegrams had arrived notifying families of the dead and wounded, but it did not affect anybody at the card games where they drank tea laced with rum and other alcoholic beverages. Yes, the war seemed far away, but even so, its breath had now reached that isolated village, and in a form that was strange, absurd, devastating.

An official order had arrived at the mayor's office, which demanded that all the Jews had to wear a six-pointed yellow star on their back and their chest. All of them, men, women and children, without distinction. Even the schoolchildren. 'Why mix them up in it?' asked Angela the midwife in bewilderment. She couldn't understand any of it. They even made a song and dance about how big the star had to be: fifteen centimetres. No smaller, so that it would be visible from a distance. How could you take them seriously?

'That's why, is it? So that it'll be visible! Very well then! Let it be visible from a distance!' Hanna said to herself, overcome with rage, when she first heard. 'I'd wear it with my head held high, proudly. In fact, I'm even going to make myself a fifteen-centimetre yellow star to put on my chest and back!' Unlike previous times, she could hardly wait for Angela to leave, and after the midwife was gone, she set to work. She searched the drawers, found a piece of yellow cloth from an old dress, cut out two six-pointed stars, and stuck them on her dress with safety-pins. She looked in the mirror. Her face was pale. She went to the door, placed her hand on the handle, as if about to go out.

'Good God, the shame! The humiliation!'

She leaned her head against the door, her hand still on the handle, not finding the strength to press it. Why this sign? Why this stigma, as if everybody were pointing at you? What had they done? They lived, struggled, breathed the same air, drank the same water as everybody else…

She thought of her parents. She pictured them walking down the street, as pale as she was now, David Kamin and Riva Kamin, both with yellow stars on their chests: they were walking side by side, holding hands, like children. Their eyes glittered, their wrinkled faces were all smiles. Like two children… Two yellow stars approaching, coming closer and closer, any minute now they would reach her, they would take her by the hand and they would continue on their way, the three of them together… She would walk between her mother and father, like when she was a little girl… But no, they walked past her, without noticing her, without pausing, even for an instant… Look, they too have yellow stars on their backs… Two yellow stars, each fifteen centimetres long, moving into the distance. They walk without looking back, without turning their eyes to see her… She wants to scream, but no sound leaves her lips. She wants to run after them, her legs won't obey her, they are rooted to the spot. Why won't they look at her? After all, she has a star too, one on her chest and one on her back, yellow stars, fifteen centimetres long… She has gone outside to show herself, so that everybody will see… No, she hasn't gone outside. She stays in the house, leaning her head against the door. She is afraid. She is ashamed…

She felt her stifled tears choking her. Her eyes were burning, but still dry. Not one tear welled from between her closed eyelids…

All of a sudden, she heard the sound of feet outside, in the yard. Hanna quickly ran to the bedroom, tore the yellow patches from her dress and hid them in the drawer of the bedside table.

A few weeks later, it was also from Angela the midwife that Hanna found out about yet another official order that had arrived in the village: All the Jews had to move to Walnut Tree Lane, also known as 'Jews' Lane.' Not only the Jews from the main village, but also those from the surrounding villages. The lane was quite long and winding, the cottages were quite numerous, crowded together, but how could so many people find room to live there? How could they all fit, all the people who had for so many years been living scattered among the lanes of the main village and in the surrounding villages and hamlets? How? And why?

The questions and bewilderment of Angela the qualified midwife had no rhyme or reason, they were utterly pointless, they were incapable of halting the natural, or rather unnatural, course of events. Soon, many houses in the village and the neighbouring settlements had been vacated and that long, winding lane had filled to bursting point with women, men and children, with three or four families crowding together in every house, and in some places, even two or three families to a single room. By night, the rooms were thick with exhaled breath, and in the morning the windows and doors were flung wide to air them. The floors were scrubbed and swept to banish the spectre of contagion that haunted those overcrowded rooms. The housewives cooked food, sparingly, fearfully meting out the scanty reserves to be found in their larders. They boiled food in their yards and gardens, lighting fires made from twigs between two bricks, since the kitchens and hearths were too few for so many families. That strange prison was well guarded. At the two ends of the lane, high barbed-wire fences had been erected, guarded day and night by burly, frowning gendarmes with bushy moustaches and rifles fitted with bayonets.

In the rest of the village, and in the surrounding villages and hamlets, the windows of many houses were boarded up and the doors were locked and sealed with string and red wax. On the shuttered windows of the general store owned by Mendel Rubinhertz, the man who had once even tried to sell powdered aspirin, and on the green-painted metal door of the cloth and textiles shop, cardboard signs had been put up, which proclaimed in jagged letters with multiple exclamation marks, 'Closed!! For rent only to Aryans!!!'

But what amazed everybody was that such a cardboard sign had also been put up on the locked and sealed door of the 'Hypocrates' pharmacy: 'Closed!! For rent only to Aryans!!!'

'Who would have believed it of him, Mr Edvard Maturinski?' said Andruschka the notary public, making the sign of the cross.

'Who would have believed it?' said Elvira, his wife, shaking the chestnut curls plastered to her forehead.

The notary felt personally offended, the same as if he had caught Maturinski cheating at cards – the same Maturinski with whom he had sat at table so many times, playing poker or rummy or sixty-six or eight-nine, drinking tea laced with rum and neat rum without tea. Worse still, he felt insulted, as if he had caught him stealing from his pocket... Even though Mr Maturinski had never been asked who he was and consequently had never denied it. Nobody had ever seen him set foot in either the church or the synagogue. And he had never been asked who he was because everybody knew that Mr Edvard Maturinski was the village pharmacist, the proprietor of the 'Hypocrates', an excellent apothecary, always ready to lend a hand – more than once, Dr Halinski had asked for his advice in the matter of pharmaceutical treatments – a polite, courteous man, the village 'gallant.' And hitherto that had been quite sufficient for everybody… Nobody had demanded anything more than that, or anything different than that…

'In any event, we can't just sit here with our arms folded! We have to do something!' cried Dr Halinski, bristling. 'We're human beings, we drank together, we played cards together, we sat at the same table with him for hundreds of Sundays, for years and years!'

'Hmm, yes, that's true,' admitted the notary, after a long pause, having got over his initial disappointment. 'But I don't really see what we can do… They're the ones who have made it their business…'

'And all we can do is soil our trousers!'

'How can you talk like that, Andrei!' Mrs Halinski exclaimed, trying to quell her husband, tugging his sleeve.

On seeing the doctor's furious eyes, which framed a nose that seemed to have grown sharper than ever, Andruschka the notary, being a man with official connections, took it upon himself to see what could be done…

But nothing could be done. Making cautious enquiry, the notary discovered that there was something unclear as to Maturinski's origins, it was impossible to establish with any precision the percentage of Aryan and non-Aryan blood that flowed in his veins – Mr Maturinski had proudly and categorically refused to provide any official document to that effect. 'He didn't want to produce any official document!' he told his secretary at the prefecture. 'And he even spoke to the commandant of the gendarmes in a haughty, ironic tone, and so they brought him under escort into town for investigation. They held him in the prison for a while, then they put him with the others in the town ghetto.' It was therefore now out of the hands of the notary, of the mayor, of the chief of the village gendarme station.

Nothing could be done.

The village seemed deserted, cowed. It was as if the people no longer walked but crept along the main street and the lanes, making no sound, hurrying to work or to their houses. The housewives exchanged brief words in low voices when they met and then hurried away to do their shopping or to get back home. In hobnailed boots, the patrols marched down the middle of the main street, stamping the gravel. They passed only in the morning and the evening, but the echo of their boots lingered long afterward.

One day, Hanna went out to do the shopping. She had heard from a neighbour that a consignment of artificial coffee, margarine and soap had arrived at the general store, and her supplies had almost run out. She was only a few steps away from the store when suddenly she heard a strident, steely voice shout behind her: '*Halt!*'

Hanna froze.

It was an SS officer, young, blond, with a handsome round face, with white skin and rosy cheeks, like a girl's. He was stiff and proud in his bearing, his grey-green uniform was impeccably tailored, his closely fitting glossy boots gleamed.

The officer walked past her, without noticing her, and went on shouting: '*Halt! Halt! Verflucht noch einmal!* Stop, you bitch!'

'I've stopped, I've stopped, *gnädiger Herr Offizer*!' came the frightened voice of a woman.

Some fifty paces in front of Hanna stood the woman at whom the officer had been shouting. Hanna could make out her features clearly. She was short, with a thin, toil-worn face, two dark, lively eyes surrounded by dark circles. But what struck Hanna the most were the wrinkles on her forehead: three, deep, horizontal furrows, which had not relaxed for a long time, if ever. She was wearing a black headscarf, from beneath which poked a few locks of curly black hair mingled with white strands, and over her shoulders was draped a dark brown shawl, which was faded, unravelling in places, moth-eaten, threadbare. She kept unconsciously tugging that shawl, on one side and the other, as if trying to conceal beneath it the basket hanging from her right arm, and at the same time covering her rather protuberant belly. She was pregnant.

The blond young officer came to a stop in front of her.

'*Du-u-u...* you are a *jiddische, nicht wahr*? Are you not?' he said in a sarcastic voice, as if savouring his own words.

'Yes, yes, *gnädiger Herr*! Merciful mister officer!' said the woman quickly, and the furrows on her brow seemed to grow deeper.

'I suspected it as soon as I laid eyes on you,' said the officer, proud of his perspicacity. 'I can smell you from a mile off... My nose is never wrong when it comes to you lot...'

And he gave an almost benevolent smile.

'What's your name?'

'Sara-Lea... Sara-Lea Berkowitz, merciful mister officer!' And she attempted to smile back.

'Is it now? Your name is Sara-Lea? Bravo! You could hardly be called anything else! Pleased to meet you, Sara-Lea!'

The officer seemed genuinely pleased. In his voice could be sensed his satisfaction at her name not having disappointed him. It would have been exasperating had that worm been called Liza or Martha or even – you never knew how far their insolence could go – Greta... When they gave themselves German names like that, it drove him to a fury...

Up to now he had been speaking in a gentle, honeyed voice, with ironical overtones, and after he discovered the woman's name, his voice had become merry, friendly even. But all of a sudden, he frowned and yelled: 'Where's your yellow star, filthy *jiddische*?'

'I've got it! I've got it here, mister *offizer*, sewn on my coat, just as they ordered, six-pointed stars, fifteen centimetres!'

She moved her old brown shawl aside and showed him the yellow star on her chest.

'Why do you hide it under that ragged shawl, you damned bitch?'

'I didn't hide it! The order was that we sew it on our coats, not on our shawls.'

'*Halt die Schnauze!* Shut up! Shut up, woman!' yelled the officer in a fury. 'That's the only thing you have in your heads: lies, fraud, deception! Where were you going?'

'To take my husband this bottle of milk and this sweater, to keep him warm. He's in hospital, with lung disease.'

The woman showed him the basket. It was true: the basket contained nothing but a bottle of milk and a dark brown sweater, a garment that Hanna recognised from afar.

'So that's it, is it? Your husband's in the sanatorium? He's taking a cure! And how did you leave the ghetto? Who gave you permission?'

Turning pale, she made no reply.

'Nothing to say? That means you escaped!'

'No, no, I just went out. But I'm going back,' she said quickly, fearfully. 'I'm just going to give my husband these things and bid him farewell. Because they say we're going to be leaving here, that they'll be taking us to a farm somewhere, to work the land… I'm just going to bid him farewell and then I'll go back, I swear, mister *offizer*! I'm going back to the ghetto, because my children are waiting for me. I've got four children…'

'What! You have four *jiddische* and you're walking around with your belly sticking out, *verfluchte Schweinhund*! You dare to bring another filthy Yid into the world?' shouted the officer, mad with rage. He then pulled out his revolver and pointed it close to the woman's belly.

'I'll go back, if you order it,' stammered the woman, pale, trembling, 'I'll go back right away, I'm going…'

'What are you going to do?' shouted Hanna in terror, taking a few steps toward him.

The shot rang out that very same moment, loud, unnatural, shaking the air. Then, a deep silence settled over the village. For a few instants, the woman stood stiff, tense, on her two legs that were thick as tree stumps, then she collapsed backwards, slowly, limply, soundlessly, like a sack of rags. The blood suddenly erupted from her belly, like an artesian well. A few drops spattered the officer's clean, elegant uniform. The officer jumped to one side, cursing through his teeth: '*Verflucht noch einmal!* What filth!'

He took an immaculate white handkerchief from his pocket and in disgust set about dabbing his stained trousers.

Hanna quickly ran up and stooped over the woman lying lifeless on the pavement. She lifted her head. There was nothing that could be done. Hanna turned to look at the officer and said in a fury: 'Why this? What did she do to you?'

Terrified people were looking from behind their doors and the curtains in their windows. A few passers-by had stopped at a distance and were standing pressed to the walls of the houses. The officer felt the eyes fixed on him from every direction. He became angry.

'What's this? How dare you ask me questions, madam? I'm the only one here who has the right to ask questions!'

The officer looked her up and down, from head to foot.

'Who are you? What are you doing here? Are you overcome with Christian mercy for this *jiddische*? Or are you of the same race as her?'

As white as chalk, Hanna stood next to the woman's lifeless body, without saying a word.

'Speak! Why are you silent? Are you a *jiddische* too?'

Father Ignatius came around the corner, from a side lane, and after listening for a few moments, he approached with rapid steps.

'What are you talking about, officer?' he interposed. 'I know this lady, she is a good Christian, a faithful daughter of Our Lord Jesus Christ. Mrs Bistricki,' he then said, addressing her directly, 'come to confession after mass this Sunday, will you? And now, go home! Your husband, engineer Bistricki, must be waiting for you impatiently... Young husbands don't like to wait for their wives too long, they prefer them to be waiting at home with their meal ready...'

The priest said the last of this blinking, addressing his words mostly to the officer, and at the same time gave Hanna a gentle push. Hanna left.

After a few moments, the officer came to his senses and barked at the priest: 'What's this? Why do you interfere in matters that have nothing to do with you? Go and see to your church! Just you wait, we'll bring order to this anarchy!'

And he went away in a fury, his head held high, stamping his elegant, highly polished boots on the empty pavement.

The priest remained alone next to the woman's lifeless body. He murmured a prayer, and then, with a few nearby Christians, he covered her with a white sheet. They put her in the horse-drawn black hearse with silver cherubs on the corners, which the priest had sent for in the meantime, and conveyed her to the closed, guarded gate of the ghetto.

At the gate, she was turned over to the community, washed, wrapped in an immaculate white shroud, placed in a funeral casket, and hoisted on the shoulders of four sturdy men. Almost every soul in the ghetto followed behind. It was a funeral such as the poor woman could never have dreamed of, not even in the happiest moments of her life.

She was buried between three unplaned boards, the way all Jews are buried, be they old or young, rich or poor, happy or unhappy, in the graveyard on the hillside, at the end of 'Jews' lane.'

The clods of earth tumbled into the grave with a dull thud, while her eldest son, the one who wrote beautifully, with letters that were like pearls, and who could draw and do sums, read the Kaddish sobbing, the prayer for the dead, under the watchful gaze of his teacher.

That day, at lunchtime, when Theodor came home, he found the table empty, with no bread, no salt, no plates, no cutlery. Hanna was sitting at the table, her face white, her body trembling.

'What's wrong? Aren't you feeling well?' he asked in alarm.

'I have to go home, Theo!' she said softly.

'Home where? I don't understand. Your home is here, Hanna.'

'I have to go to my parents. To see them. To be with them…'

She could picture her little mother, her delicate face, and next to her, her father, with his round, chestnut beard, trimmed short, both of them carrying bundles and old, shabby suitcases, walking in a long column of silent people on their way to the ghetto. Where would the ghetto be in her town? And what will her parents have taken with them from among so many useful and useless things to be found in a house?

'I have to go, maybe they need me –'

'What can you do to help them, now, in this situation…' but Theodor abruptly fell silent. He realised that he had no arguments and that the more he spoke of 'the situation' the more determined she would be to leave. He therefore added only this: 'If you believe that it is absolutely necessary… I'll come with you, Hanna. I won't let you go alone!'

Theodor told Mr Pattunek that he needed to take a day off, that he had to go home to see his parents. He had received a letter, his mother was feeling unwell… The administrator immediately gave the order to the coachman, and early in the morning of the next day, the farm *britzka*[7] took engineer Bistritzki and his wife to the station, which was about seven kilometres from the village.

All the way, in the carriage and then in the train, they exchanged only a few inconsequential words.

'Are you cold, Hanna?'

'No, no.'

'The mornings are cold.'

'Yes, cold…'

'Would you like something to eat, Hanna?'

'No, thank you, Theodor, I'm not hungry.'

A few hours later, they arrived. Hanna looked out of the window of the train carriage. The station was unchanged: the long, one-storey building, the green pillars along the platform, the flowerless flowerpots hanging from the ceiling. An unusual sense of calm suddenly flooded Hanna; she felt relieved. Yes, the station was unchanged. Here,

---

7   Britzka - open carriage with a folding hood (Polish *bryczka*)

everything was tranquil, unchangeable. No, no! Nothing could happen in that provincial town where she had been born and had grown up. The streets were the same, the houses the same, just as she had left them a few months ago, on her departure. Had it been only a few months? Good God, it was as if years had passed since then… They were walking along the streets. Yes, the houses were the same, with their pointed roofs of tile or red sheet metal, but they seemed smaller; the streets were the same, with their cracked pavements and worn cobblestones, but they seemed narrower. There in the village, whenever her mind had travelled back, the town had seemed much larger…

Here was their house. Her heart began to thud. She rushed to the gate, went into the yard. Silence. As she was about to press the door handle, she saw above it a piece of string whose ends were encased in red wax seals.

She looked through the window of the veranda. The square table, painted light yellow, was still in the middle of the room, but it was bare, stripped of its tablecloth. The table top was empty, without a vase of flowers, with nothing but a fine layer of grey dust. She had never seen it like that before. The chairs were still there, too, around the table, but one of them had been knocked over. Hanna stood for a long time with her nose pressed to the windowpane and regarded the table, the chairs, the silence. Yes, the silence was so thick, so dense, that it was as if it were visible to her. She could feel it seeping through the walls of the house, through the windowpanes of the veranda, enveloping the street, the town, her life. She could no longer hear anything. Neither the muffled murmur of the town nor the buzzing of the bee wheeling around her.

'Let's go, Hanna,' said Theodor softly. Her prolonged silence frightened him.

Hanna did not move from the window of the veranda. She heard and felt nothing. She saw only the dusty table, the chairs, the silence. Or perhaps she no longer saw anything, the silence having engulfed all. All that remained were herself and that dense, petrified silence.

'Maybe we should go to my cousin Helena's? We could wait at her house until the train back this afternoon. You could see your friend from school again…'

Theodor spoke in a hesitant voice, seeking thereby to drive away the feeling of aloneness that suddenly gripped him.

Hanna made no answer. She did not seem to have heard anything he said.

Theodor felt alone and, even though he had been with her the whole journey, even though he had been at her side, he sensed that Hanna was alone, too. Fate had not struck them equally. He understood clearly that the sealed house, the veranda with the dust-covered table and chairs meant something different to her than they did to him. True, even to Theodor it was an absurd, desolate sight, heart-rending in its very muteness, but nonetheless, he looked at it somehow from the outside, whereas she saw things from the inside, from the depths of a childhood spent in that house, from the depths of her life thitherto.

'It would be better if we went to her house,' continued Theodor, although speaking more to himself. 'In case anybody finds out we've come…'

Hanna abruptly turned away from the window of the veranda and quickly went out into the street. Theodor followed her and took her arm.

The streets were almost empty. The few passers-by seemed to creep along, hugging close to the walls of the houses.

'Where are we going, Hanna?'

She made no reply. She walked straight ahead, turned down a side street, then down another, and emerged onto the main street in the centre of town.

'I think you're aware that there's not really any need for us to say hello to any acquaintances of ours?' Theodor went on, in the admonishing, instructional tone one might use with a child.

Hanna made no reply. Theodor soon calmed down. The main street was deserted. Here and there, a figure slipped from a shop and hurriedly vanished around a corner. A woman with a shopping bag, a man running an errand. As they walked past, the people did not look at each other, they did not acknowledge each other. 'How quiet it is!' the thought flashed through Hanna's mind. Perhaps because it was a Monday. The town was always quiet on Mondays. Or was it a Tuesday? Was it Monday or Tuesday? It couldn't be Wednesday! Out of the question! Wednesday was market day. The streets were full of people bustling back and forth, talking, gesticulating, haggling. The hawkers and the vendors with booths on the street or counters under the arched gateways shouted the tempting attributes of their wares at the top of their voices:

'Get your handsome sturdy boots here!'

'Gingerbread!'

'Mirrors! Combs!'

'The cheapest and the best, only here!'

Children filled the streets, licking red, yellow, green, blue lollipops, or biting with gaping, greedy mouths white candy floss on long thin sticks, or wandering around, their faces smeared with dark tuppence chocolate. When she was little her father used to give her a penny and she would race from the clock repair shop to buy herself a lollipop. They came in different colours, but she liked the red ones; her lips would turn red and she would look like a lady wearing lipstick.

No, no! It couldn't be a Wednesday. There were no makeshift booths, no counters under the arched gateways, no hawkers. Only a few shops were open. Many of them were shuttered. On the shutters were pasted pieces of paper that said: 'Closed! To let only to Aryans!'

But maybe it was a Wednesday, and on her father's shuttered clock repair shop there would be a piece of paper that read… She reached the side street. No! The clock repair shop was open. 'Maybe they overlooked it,' the absurd thought passed through her mind… Hanna rushed down the side street and burst inside the little shop. Everything was in its place: the clocks on the wall, of every shape and size, with their long black pendulums and brass discs or chains from which depended pinecone-shaped weights; the little workbench, with its screwdrivers and cogs and minuscule springs. But at the workbench wearing a black loupe over his eye was seated not her father, David Kamin, that short man with a round, chestnut beard. As she crossed the threshold, the man who stood up from the workbench was young, lanky, with a thin nose and very thin, blond hair. With a polite smile, he greeted her.

'How can we help you, madam?'

For a few seconds, Hanna was caught off balance.

'My watch… seems to have stopped.'

She took off her wristwatch and handed it to him.

The lanky watchmaker examined it, put it to his ear, lightly shook it, and then looked at her in amazement.

'But it's working!'

'It's slow…'

'It's not slow at all, madam!'

'Slow, fast, whatever…' said Hanna, annoyed.

'It's very accurate. See for yourself!' And he showed her the clock on the wall, the only one whose heavy brass pendulum was swinging right, left, a large, solid horologe in a rectangular case with turrets on top and a lacquered white face inscribed with elongated Roman numerals, the clock by which her father used to set his Omega pocket watch and all his customers' watches…

'Yes, it's very accurate… very accurate…' mumbled Hanna, defeated, unable to take her eyes off the clock on the wall.

The tall, blond watchmaker followed her gaze and seemed to understand.

'You seem to be looking for somebody else… Maybe you were his customer,' he said, embarrassed. Not receiving an answer, he went on in an apologetic voice: 'He wasn't here when I started… I don't even know him. There was a piece of paper that said: "Closed! To let…" I was an apprentice for three years, then a journeyman for three years, I've only just taken my master's exam, I got my certificate and I asked the Guild Association and the Town Hall for premises… so that I could open a small workshop… that's what everybody does… I'm not from around here and I didn't ask for this shop in particular!' he said, stressing the final statement. 'It was given to me! I could hardly refuse, if I'd applied for a shop, could I?'

He abruptly fell silent. Theodor had entered the shop, uneasy that Hanna was taking so long.

'How can we help you, sir?'

'I'm the lady's husband. I was waiting for her outside.'

'My apologies.'

Theodor took her by the arm. Hanna asked the watchmaker: 'Where were they taken?'

'To the brickworks… That's what I've heard said. I'm not from around here. I don't know anybody in this town!' He laid heavy emphasis on the words, as if wishing to assure them that he had nothing to do with the matter.

Hanna and Theodor quickly left.

'It's time we went back to the station. We can still catch the one o'clock express,' said Theodor.

'The brickworks. Of course. That's where the ghetto is,' thought Hanna. She could not imagine a more suitable site. They would not bother anybody out there. The noises and unpleasant smells of the crowding would not reach as far as the town. The brickworks were at the very edge of town, far from the centre. The fires of its kilns had long since gone out, its huts and buildings were empty, ramshackle. The anonymous company that owned it had gone bankrupt and since then it had fallen into disrepair.

'I have to go there, Theodor!'

'There's no point, Hanna! For a fact, it will be guarded by gendarmes and you won't be able to get in. And if you do get in, you won't be able to get back out…'

'You go to the station and wait for me there! Please, Theo, darling, go! And if I'm not back in time for the evening train, don't wait for me any longer.'

'I'm not going to leave you on your own, Hanna! You're not going to take a single step by yourself! If you go, then I'm coming with you…'

'There's no point in your coming. Please, go to your uncle's, to your cousin Helena's, or to the station, wherever you think best, and wait for me there, please!'

'I'm coming with you, Hanna! Didn't we swear that we would be together for the rest of our lives? Whatever the circumstances? Do you want me to break my oath, now of all times?' Hanna was about to answer, but Theodor peremptorily concluded: 'Please don't say another word!'

They arrived at the brickworks, having run the last part of the way, all out of breath. They came to a sudden stop, in amazement. There was no trace of any gendarmes or guards. The rusty old iron gate with new barbed wired coiled around the top hung crookedly open. Within there was a strange silence, a profound, absolute silence, a silence unusual for a place where you would expect to hear the breath and the murmur of so many people…

Within, a surprising sight: on the paths among the ramshackle buildings and huts, among the cold kilns, everywhere, paper scraps of every colour, empty tin cans, old pots, rags, broken toys, littering the ground in complete disarray. It looked as if a large number of people had been forced to abandon the place in a hurry, without having time to sweep, to tidy up after themselves…

Silence had settled over those rags and paper scraps and holey pots and broken toys. A silence that painfully pressed against the eardrums.

All of a sudden there came a slight rustling sound and a clink of metal, as if a rat were rooting among the paper scraps and tin cans on the ground. A woman emerged from a hut. A tall, thin woman whose long bony arms were like twigs. Her white, dishevelled hair poked from under a black headscarf. She was wearing a torn, grimy black dress, which was so large on her that it fluttered like a funeral banner around her thin body when she moved. She walked with her eyes on the ground, searching among the litter. She stooped, picked something up, tossed it away, carried on walking, stooped once more… When she set eyes on the two of them, she fled in fear, disappeared at the other end of the brickworks.

The oppressive, tomb-like silence once more descended on the cold kilns and the ramshackle huts and barracks…

The two of them were the only people in the waiting room at the station, sitting on a bench in the corner. There was still another hour before the last train left. Theodor looked anxiously at the clock. How slowly the time passed! It was dreadfully slow. Another fifty-nine minutes. A century had passed and still there were fifty-eight minutes before the train left. If it wasn't running late. That was all he needed. His nerves were frayed enough from waiting as it was.

To Hanna time had become completely meaningless. People care about time, they measure it, they divide it, they hurry, they are always in a hurry, but time does not care about people. Time is the greatest betrayer. That clock on the wall, with its castle turrets, with its white face covered in elongated Roman numerals, still ticked, showing the exact time in David Kamin's watch repair shop, as if nothing had happened… What did Hanna care about time?

'Fifty-three minutes,' muttered Theodor. 'An eternity! But who's that?'

A short man in a shabby railway signalman's uniform was standing in the doorway of the waiting room. His face was nothing but wrinkles and he had a large, drooping moustache. He held a grubby yellow flag wrapped around a short handle. He stood in the doorway and looked fixedly at Hanna, his small eyes blinking tensely. Hanna could not remember ever having seen him before. From outside came the whistle of a manoeuvring locomotive. The man quickly moved from the doorway, went down the platform and vanished among the railway tracks.

Uneasy, Theodor looked at the clock again. Time had obviously stopped dead. The clock was working, but time was at a standstill. He never could have imagined that an hour could be so dreadfully long.

A few minutes later, the signalman reappeared in the doorway of the waiting room. But this time he lingered for no more than a few seconds before walking over to their corner and timidly sitting down on the bench, about half a metre from Hanna. He took off his grubby cap and smoothed his sweaty black hair.

'I know you, madam. I saw you more than once in your father's watch repair shop, when you were younger. I recognised you straightaway. He used to repair this old timepiece for me, when it fell sick…'

From his pocket, he took out a large, thick pocket watch, which rested in a shiny tin case sheathed in a leather slip.

After a pause, the man continued in a lower voice: 'I was on duty at the station when they took them away in the goods trucks. Three long trains in three days. Seventy or eighty to a goods truck, with boards and barbed wire nailed over the windows. Three thousand to a train. When I saw them among the others on the loading platform, I slipped up to them to say a word. And when I came up to them, I didn't know what to say; not one word came to mind. Not "have a good journey," not "all the best," not "see you again soon." Nothing. I stood there staring like I was dumb… Then Mr Kamin asked me, with a smile, "Is the watch working all right, Mihai?" I couldn't answer him. I had a big lump in my throat and I couldn't get a single word out. Then your mammy, seeing that Mr Kamin knew me, came up to me and told me in a whisper that if I saw you… "If our daughter Hanna comes home, tell her that…"'

The signalman fell silent.

'Tell me what?' asked Hanna feverishly.

'She didn't manage to finish what she was saying. A gendarme came and yelled at them, "What are you waiting for? Get in the truck, we don't want you lingering here in our country like a bad smell…" And to me he said: "Don't you know you're not allowed to go near them or talk to them? Make yourself scarce, you bastard! Or do you want us to put you in the truck with them, so that you'll have all the time in the world to chatter?" They closed the doors, padlocked them…'

The signalman said no more. A heavy silence settled between them.

By now it was dark outside. Black shadows pooled in the corners.

'Where did they take them in those trucks?' asked Theodor.

'Nobody knows. Our lads, the mechanic and the stoker, took them as far as the border, which is where they changed locomotives. The soldiers on the other side took them from there. Our lads saw only that the trains crossed the border… Some say they were taken to some farms, to work the land, that their young men were sent to the front…'

A locomotive whistled.

'It's manoeuvring, I have to go!'

The signalman quickly got up from the bench, grasped his dirty yellow flag, went out onto the platform, and melted away among the dimly lit railway tracks.

It was silent in the waiting room once more. Hanna's eyes felt parched, her cheeks were burning. She began to tremble, her teeth chattering. Theodor placed his palm on her forehead.

'You've got a temperature, Hanna.'

He took off his raincoat and wrapped her in it. He looked at the clock. It would only be a few more minutes before the train left.

That gunshot, which had felled the pregnant wife of Berkovitz the tailor on the main street of the village in broad daylight, did not remain without consequences.

Before three days were out, Father Ignatius received a telephone call from the bishop's secretary, inviting him to present himself before His Holiness the next day, on Saturday morning.

His Holiness was summoning him, a humble village priest? To present himself before him? Why? It could only be for the good. There was no other explanation. His zeal, his piety, his good works had at last been noticed.

As he always did at important moments in his life, Father Ignatius made a thorough examination of his conscience. He had never fallen prey to the Devil, unlike other mortals and even other village priests of weaker fibre, who were unable to resist temptation or even the boredom of dull, monotonous village life; he had never succumbed to drink or tobacco or other diabolical pleasures; he had never touched a playing card, not even with his fingertip, and he did not have a young housekeeper…

No! He had not disregarded a single jot of God's Word! He had not allowed temptation and boredom and sloth to make their nest in his heart. The whole time he had ardently studied the holy books, he had preached the Lord's teachings and brought comfort and hope to people's souls.

He abruptly stopped. The wind no longer filled his sails. And he grew afraid… He was afraid to rejoice… Might the Lord be putting him to the test?

'Yes! Thee, Ignatius, His lowliest and most insignificant servant,' he said to himself, pointing an accusing finger in his mind. 'Just as He put the righteous and unblemished Job to the test through suffering, might He not put thee to the test through joy, through praise? Might He not thereby test the mettle of thy soul, thy piety, thy humility? See how pride and conceitedness and excess have made their nest in thy soul…'

Father Ignatius began to murmur, as in prayer: 'Vanity of vanities, saith Ecclesiastes, vanity of vanities! All is vanity. I said in my heart, Go to now, I will prove thee with mirth, therefore enjoy pleasure:

and behold, this is also vanity. I said of laughter, It is mad, and of mirth, what doeth it? Vanity of vanities.'

But no matter how many times Father Ignatius repeated the words, pouring cold water on his burning head, he still felt his heart full of joy, a joy he could not quell.

'No, Lord God! Thou who seest all and nothing is hidden from Thy face, and who readest my heart like an open book, Thou knowest that of the little that I have done, I have done nothing to deserve praise or any reward in this world…'

What he did on the village main street now crossed his mind. Maybe it had reached the ears of His Holiness… He had saved a good and merciful Christian, a daughter of Christ, from the claws of the Antichrist. For only an antichrist could shoot a pregnant woman in the blessed womb. An antichrist and emissary of Hell! The blood rushed to his cheeks as he remembered the scene. A pity the Lord had not quickened his steps so that he could have arrived in time to save the poor Jewess too. He had heard the gunshot from a distance and when he turned the corner into the street, he saw the woman lying in a pool of blood, and the young Mrs Bistricki bending over her, like the true merciful Christian she was, like a worthy daughter of Him who was crucified to redeem the sins of mankind. Why had the Lord not quickened his steps? Or maybe He had deliberately not done so? Could it be true that that some people had been chosen for torment and suffering? Always to redeem their sins and others'? 'If thou wilt not obey the voice of thy Lord God, and if thou wilt not seek to abide by His commandments and laws, then all these curses will come down upon thee. Cursed wilt thou be in the city, cursed in the plain, cursed will be thy womb and the fruit of thy womb… Thy sons and thy daughters will be given unto another nation and thy eyes will dissolve in tears for mourning them by day and by night and of strength wilt thou be bereft… A nation that thou knowest not will eat the fruit of thy earth and all thy labours, and all thy days wilt thou be downtrodden…'

'No! No!' exclaimed Father Ignatius in horror. He quickly closed the leather-bound Bible in front of him, stood up from his chair and began to pace up and down the stark, whitewashed room whose walls showed nothing but a dark wooden cross, which hung to the east. 'No! No! In that way we descend into the deepest darkness, whence there is no egress… In that way, we end up justifying every crime and atrocity… Even so, we have been given the power of heart and mind, to be able to choose between good and evil. Nobody has the right knowingly to pose as the avenging arm of God Above and to translate into terrible deeds His intentions, which none do know…'

Having thus removed the seed of doubt that had attempted to lodge in his soul, the priest placed a fragment of soap, a rough towel and a prayer book in his valise and went to bed.

He slept peacefully for a few hours.

At dawn the next day, a Saturday, Father Ignatius set off cheerfully, with an easy heart, walking the seven kilometres to the station. He went on foot for three reasons, as he liked to say. Firstly: That was how the Apostles themselves travelled. Although he was sorry that he, unworthy man that he was, wore very comfortable soft black leather shoes, polished to a sheen by his assiduous old housekeeper, whereas the Apostles went mostly barefoot, with the hot dust of the road scorching the soles of their feet, with the torrid sun burning their brows, or with the sticky mud hindering their steps in rainy weather. More often than not, their feet were covered in bleeding wounds because of sharp stones, spiny weeds, stinging nettles, thorns… And they didn't walk just seven kilometres, but to the ends of the Earth, tireless and persecuted, so that they might bear witness to Our Lord. Secondly: he walked to the station because he did not wish to spend parish funds on a horse and trap or to bother a peasant from the village or the overseer from the estate to take him by cart free of charge… And thirdly: he was accustomed to walking. After all, he walked for even longer distances to the outlying villages and hamlets of his parish, crossing hill and dale to officiate at baptisms, weddings and funerals. He liked to walk, to gaze upon the proud works of nature, the clear, endless blue of the sky, the verdant land, the blossoming orchards, to listen to the fresh matutinal song of the birds and the peasants greeting each other as they went to work in the fields:

'Praise be…'

'Forever and ever, amen…'

Arriving at the station, he bought his ticket and boarded a third-class carriage. Again, there were three reasons for this. When he was alone, he liked to converse with himself and provide solid reasons for his actions. Firstly: He could not countenance pointless expenditure of church money. Secondly: He did not permit himself any luxury, not even on his own money. 'My own money,' the priest said to himself with a smile. 'What a euphemism! When all money is the devil's…' And thirdly: He travelled third class because he took every opportunity to mingle with the poor.

At the bishopric, he did not have to wait very long in the vast, empty antechamber, which was furnished with nothing but chairs upholstered in black leather along the walls and a dark red velvet carpet in the middle of the parquet floor, on which trod high prelates and important lay persons as they entered and departed with solemn, preoccupied faces. Father Ignatius remained standing in the corner by the entrance for a few minutes, after which he was ushered into the bishop's office.

It was a spacious room soberly furnished with an imposing desk of solid ebony and a high-backed armchair, on which His Holiness was seated. In front of the desk were two chairs with lower backs, upholstered in the same black leather. On the walls hung a few oil paintings of bishops past.

The bishop was a tall, thin man with a deeply furrowed, energetic face. A fluff of sparse white hair framed his head like a halo. Father Ignatius made a deep bow before him.

'I have summoned you, my son…' began the bishop, in a deep, gentle voice, and then paused, as if pondering how to continue.

'It is a great honour for me to be able to appear before Your Holiness!' said Father Ignatius, making use of the bishop's pause to say aloud the words he had prepared at home and had been rehearsing over and over again in his mind. He now recited those words in the modest, humble, respectful tone of voice suited to such an occasion.

'It is a great honour for me, the priest of a small parish –'

'We are aware of your zeal and devotion in the service of the Church and enlightenment of the faithful, my son!' interrupted the bishop and with a weary gesture invited him to be seated.

A warmth enveloped the priest on hearing these words. It was as he had presupposed: He had been noticed, his work was known and appreciated.

'You are still young, Father Ignatius. How old are you?' asked the bishop, wrinkling his brow.

'Thirty-nine, Your Holiness, fifteen years of which I have spent in the service of the Holy Church.'

'Thirty-nine… thirty-nine years old…' murmured the bishop, studying the priest's face. Framed by thick, chestnut hair, worn swept back, that face, with its slightly hooked nose and deep, dark, blinking eyes, conveyed a naïve, almost fanatical enthusiasm.

'That must be what I looked like when I was thirty-nine,' thought the bishop to himself, 'when I was a priest in that wretched country parish and the Great War broke out, which, from there in the village, I tried to stop, fervently preaching universal peace from the pulpit…' And he smiled to himself, enveloping in a warm, sympathetic gaze the young priest who sat shyly, stiffly on the edge of the upholstered chair before him.

But nothing of these thoughts could be read on the bishop's grave face when a few moments later he continued: 'Hmm, you are still young. A great responsibility rests on your shoulders. And youth and zeal sometimes make you cross certain boundaries, without your realising…'

The priest gave a start. He did not understand. Or had he not heard aright? What forbidden boundaries had he crossed?

'Forgive me, but I do not understand, Your Holiness…'

'I have received a complaint against you. I say 'complaint,' but in fact it is more a vehement protest on the part of the German Command. An officer, by the name of –' here the bishop cast a glance at the piece of paper lying on the desk in front of him '– SS-Hauptsturmführer Walther von Klopfnagel complains that you do not limit yourself to church activities but interfere in secular, political matters –'

'But the officer shot a pregnant woman in the middle of the street, in broad daylight, in my parish!'

'It says here, "a disobedient Jewess".'

'Is that what it says? 'Disobedient'?'

"Which has nothing to do with the Christian religion and Church servants should not interfere –"

'But the man who shot the pregnant Jewess calls himself a Christian! And in the Ten Commandments it says, "Thou shalt not kill"! It does not say who should not kill or whom we should not kill, only "Thou shalt not kill"! In other words, nobody should kill anybody…'

Father Ignatius had unwittingly raised his voice, filled with increasing irritation and forgetting for a moment whom he was addressing. When he remembered, he abruptly fell silent, frightened. But the bishop regarded him calmly, solemnly, in silence.

'Please forgive me, Your Holiness… In any case, I didn't interfere for the sake of that unfortunate Jewess. Unfortunately, I arrived too late to be able to do anything… However, I did save a Christian from the hands of that officer, a merciful woman who leapt to the aid of the woman who was shot. I explained that I knew her, that she was a faithful daughter of Christ, that she was the wife of engineer Bistricki –'

'The lay authorities could have done that!' The bishop made a gesture of annoyance. 'The town hall could have provided proof of who she was, what she was, reinforced by signatures and rubber stamps!'

The priest was thunderstruck. In other words, it meant that he had achieved nothing. It meant that what he thought had been a good deed was nothing of the sort, even quite the contrary, it would seem. But whoever was there and had seen the situation, whoever had seen the officer's blind rage and rashness, would have realised… Who knows if there would have been time for the matter to have reached the town hall…

'You see, my son,' the bishop went on, in a gentle, paternal voice, 'the spires of the Church soar to the heavens, but her foundations are on earth… At the present time, we can do nothing but pray. We must ceaselessly raise our fervent prayers to the Lord Above, but we must not interfere in worldly matters, in their politics. We must not give the godless an opportunity to harm the Holy Church! Let us therefore avoid any conflict with them, who are the unwitting instruments of Heaven –'

'Or of Hell!' interrupted Father Ignatius, outraged.

'Or of Hell, as you rightly say, my son,' said the bishop with a smile. 'This is precisely why we must keep as far away from them as possible.'

'I see in them the Antichrist,' continued the priest, encouraged.

'Antichrists or the hand of the Lord, Who punishes sins… I don't know. We cannot know. Our minds are too limited for us to be able to fathom all the Creator's secrets and intentions… but what we do know for certain is that we must think not only of saving certain people, but of saving the Church above all else. We must think of how to shepherd the Church unvanquished and unblemished through these times of wrath and peril… Do you understand, Father Ignatius?'

The priest nodded. He understood, of course he did. After all, the words sounded only too clear and categorical in the mouth of the bishop.

But even so, he did not understand. Were not good deeds and saving people the pillars on which rested the Church? He had come there hoping to receive praise and he had been given a reprimand. A gentle, paternal reprimand, obviously, but for what? Because the urging of his heart and the modest lights of his mind had led him to do a Christian deed?

'And be more temperate in your words, my son, in the beautiful, passionate sermons you preach from the pulpit on Sundays. Avoid any allusion to… Above all any overly transparent allusion…'

'But I have not made any allusions whatever, Your Holiness,' said the priest, in genuine astonishment. The bishop again cast his eyes over the closely typed piece of paper in front of him, seeking the relevant passage, and began to read.

"We are overcome with fear… Many have come to conceal their clean thoughts… Parents who must hide from the children they have begotten. Brothers forced to part from their brothers in thought and deed… This is why it is meet that we cry out in the words of St John: 'Little children, it is the last time, and as ye have heard that antichrist shall come, even now are there many antichrists…'"

The bishop looked further down the page.

'"They went out from us, but they were not of us… but they went out, that they might be made manifest that they were not all of us… He is antichrist, that denieth the Father and the Son." Do you recognise the words, my son?'

'I recognise them!' answered the priest, in fear and amazement.

'And it goes on, word for word, letter for letter…'

Did it mean that ears were listening and a hand was writing down everything he uttered in his own church?

'But I was speaking more generally, I wasn't referring to anybody in particular!'

'But they took it to refer to them.'

'All the better!' blurted the priest. 'It means the words were not wasted!'

'No, it's not better at all, my son! Not at all!' answered the bishop, raising his voice in annoyance for the first time. 'Just now, you said you understood, but it is plain that you did not understand. They did not take it as a lesson, but as instigation against them! And we must not draw down their blind rage upon us. As long as they leave the Lord's Church in peace…'

The priest listened, pale-faced, blinking uneasily. After a pause, the bishop continued in a calmer voice.

'What are you going to speak about in your sermon tomorrow?'

'The Sixth Commandment. "Thou shalt not kill."'

'Also without making any allusions?' the bishop asked, ironically.

'No! I picked the subject deliberately,' confessed Father Ignatius. 'After what happened in my parish, in the middle of the street, in broad daylight.'

'I would advise you to change the subject! Why not talk about the First Commandment: "I am the Lord God. Thou shalt have no other gods before Me."' The bishop hesitated for a moment. 'Or better still, the last commandment, the tenth: "Thou shalt not covet thy neighbour's house, thou shalt not covet thy neighbour's wife, nor his manservant,"' the bishop paused again, grew angry. 'Or even better still, leave out the Ten Commandments just this once and, since they have their eyes on everything you do and their ears on everything you say, talk about Judas' betrayal… Or if you don't feel up to it, give up the sermons for now. The Church must be able to admonish and chastise, to thunder and fulminate. But also to suffer in silence… To all things their time and place. Do you understand, my son?'

The priest nodded once again. He understood, of course he did. After all, the bishop's words were clear. But even so, he did not really understand… He had once again received a reprimand, for what he had thought would be well deserving of praise. For that sermon…

In his mind, Father Ignatius continued the conversation even after he made a deep, respectful bow before the bishop and backed out of his spacious office. He continued the conversation, asking His Holiness questions and supplying the answers in his stead, as he walked to the station and as he sat in the third-class carriage on his way home… We must save the Church! Of course… But did not the Church rise up in times of trouble to lift the fallen, to shelter the displaced, to succour the oppressed? Should it not show its courage and generosity, now of all times? We must not interfere in worldly matters, in politics! Yes, it is true, we are not statesmen or politicians. But precisely because we are not, we are able to say things that politicians cannot and will not say… We even must remind them of certain things! We have no right to be silent, when the time comes to speak out… The prophets did not hold their tongues! Our Lord Jesus Christ did not hold his tongue! Father Ignatius suddenly felt anger and indignation swelling in him. We must not interfere in secular matters, but they have the right to interfere in Church matters… they send pagan ears to spy on us and sinful hands to write down word for word everything that is said from the pulpit. They advise us on what we should and should not say! No! Nobody has the right! And here the priest thought to hear the indignant voice of the bishop: We must not draw down on the Church their suspicion and blind, destructive fury. But perhaps the bishop was right. They had brute force and knew no scruple whatever. Where had such creatures sprung from? In the middle of the street, in the clear light of day, I saw what they are capable of. They don't even need the darkness of night to conceal their evil deeds, unlike common criminals… But if they close our churches and drive us from our altars and pulpits, where will we preach the truth? Where will we make the Lord's word heard? What if they close our churches? What if they demolish them? I saw how quick they are to draw their pistols, we may suppose they are just as quick when it comes to firing cannons…

Father Ignatius shuddered as he sat on the hard, wooden bench of the third-class carriage. Then, overcome by the exhaustion of that hard day and the sweltering heat in the train compartment, he drifted off to sleep, rocked by the puffing, rattling, rhythmically creaking train as it took him back to the village.

After the young priest, so full of zeal, ardour, and bodily and spiritual vigour had bidden him farewell, making a deep bow and respectfully backing out of his office, the bishop said to himself: 'How simple it all is for him! How easy! There in the village, he has peace and quiet, fresh air, pure water, natural scenery... He serves at the altar, preaches on Sundays, officiates baptisms, weddings, funerals... And when something happens... a gunshot rings out... just one! In the peace and quiet of the village, the echo is deafening. The world is turned upside down... But even so, maybe that young priest is right. Maybe we should let them close our churches. Let them demolish them, even, and let us go out into the street to cry out the word of the Lord at the top of our voices! Let us admonish and chastise evil and lawlessness! Without fear of anybody or anything. Let us follow the example of the Prophets! And the example of Our Lord Jesus Christ!'

And the bishop once again saw himself as a young, zealous priest in that dusty, rickety village at the ends of the earth, where folk had been shepherds since time immemorial. A shot had rung out then, too, far away, in Sarajevo, and its echo had carried all the way to his parish. War had broken out. And he, too, from the small pulpit of his wooden church had preached universal peace... And goodwill among men and all the nations. He had cried out that they cast aside their guns. That they stop killing each other. That they melt down their rifles and cannons and battlewagons and forge them into ploughshares, so that the vision of the Prophet Isaiah might at last be fulfilled...

He, too, had been summoned to the bishopric... like Father Ignatius now. He had expected to be praised...

'*Eyn hadash tahat hashemesh*,' the bishop had said, repeating the words of wise Solomon in the original Hebrew. 'Nothing is new under the sun.' And warmth suddenly flooded the aged soul of the bishop, who had never had children, apart from those of the Church. He felt like sending for the young priest, summoning him back, or better still, he felt like getting up and running after him, embracing him, praising him, kissing him, saying, 'You did well, my son! You did well! I am proud of you!'

But he could not. He was bound by his high office. It was as if he were pinned to that large, sumptuous, ebony desk and that high-backed armchair… And besides, he did not have time: he had to write a reply to the protest from the German Command. A dignified reply, which would very determinedly reject their interference in Church matters, but couched in choice, gentle, conciliatory words, so as not to annoy or provoke them…

And that was no easy matter.

The bishop called for his secretary, to dictate to him…

That Saturday, while Father Ignatius was at the bishopric, a military car came to a stop in front of the sanatorium, three kilometres outside the village.

From the car alighted three officers in grey-green uniforms. A young, blond officer with a round face and girlishly white skin and two sub-officers. Holding his head high, the officer marched to the director's office, followed by the other two. Three pairs of boots stamped rhythmically down the stone-floored corridor.

Dr Halinski, the sanatorium director, received them with a polite smile, rising from his desk. Small, thin, his pointed nose reached only as high as the officer's shoulder.

The officer held his arm aloft and uttered a cold, steely 'Heil Hitler!'

The two sub-officers repeated his gesture and barked in the same tone, 'Heil Hitler!'

'Good day!'

'I am SS-Haupsturmführer Walther von Klopfnagel.'

'Highly honoured! I am Dr Halinski.'

'We have been informed that you are concealing Jews in this hospital.'

'In this hospital we don't conceal anybody. We house people, people suffering from pulmonary tuberculosis, whom we treat and try to cure, Herr… führer.'

'Hauptsturmführer!' the officer corrected him, wrathfully.

'I apologise, Herr Hauptsturm…'

'… führer!'

'That's what I said!'

'To be specific, Herr Direktor: Do you know a *Jude*, a tailor by the name of Chaim Berkovitz?'

'No, I don't. I know a seriously ill man, with bilateral tuberculosis… I don't care what his name is or what size shoes he wears, Herr… Sturmführer.'

'Haupsturmführer!' the officer corrected him, offendedly.

'Herr Haupt…'

'… sturmführer!'

'That's what I said,' muttered the doctor.

'Anyway, you will surrender this *Jude* to us! And immediately!'

'No patient will be surrendered to anybody so long as I am director of this hospital.'

'What? Do you know whom you are talking to? We shall have to speak to your superiors, Herr Direktor!'

'As for that, I have no other superiors than my conscience, Herr Haupt – Sturm – Führer,' said the doctor, stressing each syllable. 'When I received my medical diploma, I swore an oath. And I have no mind to break it, not for anybody! We receive patients in this hospital to cure them, not to send them away still sick or to surrender them.'

The officer was momentarily caught off balance. He had not been expecting such defiance and he had arrived unprepared. He had thought it would be enough for him to give the order. His girlishly white face flushed and between gritted teeth he said, 'I shall return very soon, Herr Direktor! And when I do, we shall talk on a different footing. Heil Hitler!'

The two sub-officers mechanically repeated his salute and shouted, 'Heil Hitler!'

The officer turned on his heel and holding his head high marched stiffly from the office, with his underlings following like a double shadow.

The three pairs of boots once more stamped rhythmically down the stone-floored corridor. The rumble of the car engine made itself heard outside, fading into the distance. The echoes finally scattered and silence descended on every corner of the sanatorium.

After he closed the door behind the soldiers, Dr Halinski began to pace up and down agitatedly, almost bumping into the walls of his small office, which was two by three metres square and furnished with only a desk and a couple of enamelled white chairs.

He was enraged.

'What cheek! What impertinence! Am I supposed to take a sick man from his hospital bed and surrender him just like that? A man who has a cavern the size of a walnut in his left lung and the beginnings of an infiltration in his right, who is burning with a pernicious, persistent low fever… What are they thinking!'

How strange, he thought, remembering the figure the young officer cut: elegant, mannered, cold. He probably has a university degree in some humanities subject. A white, round face, like a girl's, in odd contrast with his stiff, deliberately masculine attitude… He could picture him pulling on his glacé gloves, his long, delicate fingers pulling the pistol from its holster, firing in the blink of an eye, without stopping to think, then placing the pistol back in its leather sheath, brushing a speck of dust from his immaculate uniform, before going off to listen to a Beethoven concert in a rapture… And the other two, who followed him like a double shadow, faceless, impersonal: try as he might, the doctor could not remember their faces, only the salute they made in the exact same moment, as if both triggered by the same spring, jerking their arms aloft and releasing from their throats that bark in perfect unison… Whence did such creatures arise? What kind of parents raised them? What kind of school educated them?

Dr Halinski came to an abrupt halt in the middle of his office. He had given them a categorical refusal. Very good! He could hardly do otherwise. Nor had he admitted that the man they were looking for was in the hospital. Also very good. But let's not be naïve! The situation is not so simple. That young officer said he would return very soon. And that lot are in the habit of keeping such promises… Punctuality, thoroughness, precision… and order! They have to have order!

In any case, something had to be done. And quickly too! But what? Should he hide him somewhere, so that when they returned, probably in greater force and with written orders from who knows what higher authority, they wouldn't find him there in the hospital… Hiding him was easier said than done. Where could you hide a sick, contagious man who needed to stay in a room kept at a constant temperature, to receive daily treatment and medication, pneumothorax every second day, and to be X-rayed at least once every three days?

There was a soft, timid knock on the door.

The doctor gave a start. But it was only the head nurse coming to ask whether the director would be doing his scheduled rounds today. It was nine o'clock… five past…

What a question! Of course he would be doing his rounds. He had no reason not to! Dr Halinski buttoned his white coat, forced himself to put on a cheerful, well-disposed mien, and visited each ward in turn.

Whatever troubles or annoyances Dr Halinski might have had, he was in the habit of 'leaving them outside the patient's door and not entering the room with them,' as he always told his assistants, the junior doctors and nurses. 'When you go in to see a patient, you must always be, or appear to be, cheerful and well-disposed.' He was of the conviction that a bad mood on the part of the doctor or nurse would be passed on to the patient, hindering his recovery.

Tuberculosis patients in particular were so preoccupied with their illness and so sensitive that if they saw a frown on the doctor's face they immediately misinterpreted it and thought it applied to them: 'Aha, the doctor knows something but he doesn't want to tell me.'

For this reason, the doctor advised his assistants that neither a quarrel with the wife, nor a lost card game the night before, nor bad news from relatives or in the papers – and there was plenty of that, what with the war spreading everywhere and no end in sight – nor a turn for the worse in the patient's condition should ever be visible on the physician's face. Yes, the doctor had to be able to playact, to hide his true feelings…

Dr Halinski therefore entered the wards with a radiant face, cracking little jokes with this and that patient.

'What's with that sour look, old man?' he asked a young man with a pallid face and dark, sunken eyes. 'Head up! Chest out! I know you inside and out, after all. I saw your X-rays just yesterday. You've got no cause to pull a face like that! It's calcifying… calcifying…'

'Slowly, doctor. All too slowly…'

'Yes, but surely!'

At the bedside of another patient, an unshaven, slovenly, irritable, middle-aged man, the doctor shook his head, half-joking, half-serious: 'We're at a standstill… Like a train stuck in a station. And do you know why? Because you won't help us to cure you. We can only do so much, but you have to lend us a helping hand too. Why don't you take your postprandial rest? We have to lie down, relaxed, even if we can't sleep…'

In ward seven, with two long rows of beds, in the right-hand corner at the end, was the bed of Chaim Berkovitz, the poor tailor. Small and thin, with a haggard face, greenish-yellow parchment-like skin, small, brown eyes framed by bluish rings, locks of black and grey hair poking from beneath his white bonnet and plastered down his broad, shiny, sweat-beaded brow, he was sitting doubled up in bed, as if bowed over an invisible needle, concentrating on an invisible seam…

'Oho! Aren't we looking good today!' said Dr Halinski cheerfully as he reached his bed.

'Yes, yes! We're looking good… Both of us, doctor!' he answered, with a sour smile.

Dr Halinski gave a start. Might he suspect something? Despite his best efforts, had he been unable to conceal his anxiety and bad mood? You could never be sure with this patient. He had given strict orders to all the staff, from the doctors to the gatekeeper, not to bring any bad news from the outside, not to pass on rumours, not to give the patients newspapers, but only novels, only science-fiction. Nonetheless, although the hospital was isolated, although it was three kilometres to the first inhabited house in the village, he could not keep it hermetically sealed; rumours still slipped through the cracks, some patients received visitors, there were chinks in the fence, plenty of loose tongues… But with this man, the tailor Berkovitz, with whom he liked to converse, to banter, to engage in mutual ribbing, it was never clear to the doctor, he was never sure what he had found out, what he knew, what he was hiding from him…

Dr Halinski therefore pretended not to pick up on the allusion and continued in an even more relaxed and cheerful tone of voice, although this time with painstaking care to avoid the first-person plural he usually employed when talking to patients.

'You really do look better, Mr Berkovitz! You even look like you've started to put on weight.'

'If you're always pestering me to eat, doctor! To eat, to stuff myself, to put some flesh on my bones. You probably want me to end up sitting next to the big, pious rabbis up there in heaven…'

'I don't understand…' said the doctor, genuinely puzzled.

The tailor gave a sly wink. 'If you have a little time, doctor…'

Dr Halinski gladly sat down on the white chair next to the patient's bed, ready to listen. He knew that Chaim Berkovitz often spoke in riddles and parables.

'They say that once, but only once, impelled by vainglory, the great and wise Rabbi Israel, known as the Bal-Shem-Tov, that is, the One-with-Good-Name, was very curious to find out whom he would sit next to there, in the next world, the heaven of the righteous... The Lord pointed at a common man, a coarse, unmannered man, an *am-haaretz*, a man with no book-learning, who was sitting at a table, eating... Eating, I say? He was stuffing himself! It was as if his only care, his only goal in life was to guzzle, to put as much flesh on his bones as he could... The great Bal-Shem was astounded. What? Next to that coarse, illiterate, vulgar, fat man he was to sit in the next world? What merits could such a man have? Impatient to solve the mystery, he went to the man and asked him why he ate so much, what was the point of getting fat when our wise men since time immemorial have said: "The more the flesh on you, the more the food for the worms." The man then told him that once, when he was still a small, frail lad, a pogrom had broken out. His father had taken him by the arm and he had tried to flee to the forest with him so they could hide. But the bad men caught him and burned him. His father was a thin, withered man and he burned quickly, the fire did not take long over him and didn't give off much light, and so people didn't have time to notice. Him they forgot, since he was so small and frail. But seeing how they burned his father, he decided to eat plenty, to get fat, to put as much flesh on his bones as he could, so that when they burned him, he would burn for a long time and with a bright flame, for all to notice, for all to see...'

The tailor suddenly fell silent. Dr Halinski felt a lump rise in his throat. For a fact, that thin, sickly man knew much more than he appeared to... or perhaps over the course of time he had developed a certain sense for approaching danger, even if he did not know from which direction it was coming... In any event, something had to be done. But what?

As he moved from bed to bed, cracking little jokes left and right, behind which he concealed his anxiety, he finally seemed to find a solution...

Dr Halinski quickly finished his rounds and ordered the coachman to harness the horse to the hospital's two-wheel buggy. He went straight to the town hall. Mr Andruschka the notary was in his office.

'What's wrong, doctor? You're pale.'

The doctor recounted to him the visit he had received from the young officer with the round, mild, girlish face and the two faceless sub-officers – he could not for the life of him remember what they looked like – and concluded: 'We have to do something, don't you think?'

'But what can we do?' asked the notary, giving a resigned shrug.

'I'm thinking that if the tailor had a different name and different parents, nobody would have anything against him, would they?'

'Naturally not!' said notary Andruschka with a laugh. 'But the thing is, he had the bad luck to have his own parents and to be called Chaim… Chaim Berkovitz.'

'But the name isn't glued to him!' exclaimed Dr Halinski, becoming annoyed. 'It's not glued to his nose or his forehead or his cheeks! If he had papers with some commonplace name… an Aryan name…'

'But that's dangerous!' said the notary, his eyes bulging.

Halinski jumped up, as if butting him with his eyes and sharp nose: 'Eating fish is dangerous too! You can choke on a bone. Eating sausages is dangerous. You can get food poisoning. Walking down the street in the middle of the day is dangerous. A loose brick can fall on your head.'

'Hey, don't get so angry!' said the notary, trying to placate him, meanwhile adjusting the wooden leg of the table. 'I was just trying to draw your attention to whether it's worth running such a risk for a… for just one… we can't save them all, even so…'

'If every person saved just one…'

The notary wiped his sweating bald patch, arranged the tufts of ginger hair above each ear, and after a pause, grumbled: 'Let me see what can be done, doctor. It's not so simple… In legal terms, it's what is called falsifying public records. You need to give me a little time, to think about how to go about it…'

'But think quickly! While your brains can still be of use. Because we haven't got very long... Look, today is Saturday, tomorrow Sunday, and hopefully they'll leave us in peace, so now's the time for us to act, and on Monday morning they'll find Berkovitz the tailor moved to the third floor, to a different ward, where nobody knows him, and under a different name...'

But the whole of this heated discussion was soon to prove completely pointless. And there was to be no need for notary Andruschka to wrack his brains or forge any document...

SS officer Walther von Klopfnagel kept his word. Not two days passed. His first visit was on Saturday, on Sunday all was quiet, as the hospital director had foreseen, and on Monday morning he presented himself at the director's office once more.

But this time the officer arrived with two vehicles, one of which was a black van, whose small windows had bars on them, and he was accompanied by a patrol of eight SS soldiers.

'Heil Hitler!'

Dr Halinski rose from his desk without a word.

The officer triumphantly laid a piece of paper on the desk. Without casting a glance at the piece of paper, Dr Halinski pressed a buzzer. An attendant entered, a tall, burly man with a black moustache.

'Josif, take the officer to Chaim Berkovitz.'

The officer and the soldiers followed the attendant. Their boots stomped rhythmically down the stone-floored corridors. They entered a cold, dark room. Chaim Berkovitz the tailor was stretched out on a slab, covered with a white sheet. He had been dead for twenty-four hours.

'Verflucht noch einmal!' muttered the officer between his teeth. And he angrily went out, followed by the soldiers.

What had happened was this: On Sunday morning, he had talked to Dr Halinski, and that afternoon he had developed a temperature. The fever grew. A runaway temperature. He passed away during the night.

Thin and dry, Chaim Berkovitz the tailor had burned quickly, all unobserved…

That Sunday, the day after his visit to the bishopric, Father Ignatius officiated mass as usual, but his voice, once so warm, full and clear, seemed weary, clouded. After the service, he climbed up to the pulpit to deliver his sermon. Up there he was solemn, tall, imposing, his swept-back chestnut hair slightly ruffled. The congregation that packed the church could see his face was tortured; sleeplessness had left dark rings around his eyes. His sermon did not flow smoothly, like a long, unstoppable river, but was punctuated with pauses and hesitations. The priest seemed to be searching for the right word, he stumbled, started a sentence only to abandon it and pursue a different idea… Nothing like it had ever happened to him before…

The sermon too was much shorter than ever before and, unlike his other sermons, people did not really understand what he wanted to say. He spoke of Judas, of his betrayal, of the thirty pieces of silver… And it flashed through his mind: Here in this church there is a traitor. Somebody was secretly listening to him, lucidly, coldly, devoid of piety, taking note of his every gesture, his every word, his every movement. And he looked down at the nave, where the congregants sat motionless in the rows of pews… Which might it be? Perhaps that young man with the tousled hair in the pew at the back? Or that middle-aged man sitting by himself in the fifth pew? He appeared to be a stranger, or else he could not see him clearly enough… You had no way of knowing. They were all listening, they all kept their hands hidden below the back of the pew in front. He could not see the congregants' hands from up there in the pulpit. He could see only their heads and shoulders. And in a vengeful voice, he found himself speaking of the repentance and death of the traitor: 'I have sinned in that I have betrayed the innocent blood… And he cast down the pieces of silver in the temple, and departed, and went and hanged himself.' All of a sudden, he stopped, overcome with anger.

This too might be misinterpreted. They might take it to refer to them. He quickly changed his tone and the subject. He spoke of Christian mercy. 'Blessed are they that mourn, for they shall be comforted. Blessed are the meek, for they shall inherit the earth.' The priest fell silent once more, frightened. This too might be understood differently… He was gripped by a choking fury. In the end, each could interpret the words however he liked, however he felt, however he thought. Was not this the whole point of a sermon? It made each congregant think in accordance with his own deeds, his own thoughts, his own measure. Was not the point of a sermon to stir, to rectify, to pain, to comfort? Then why should we be afraid of people, if the Lord is with us? And he felt like shouting: 'Go home, good folk! The world is broken! There is no longer any point in coming to church!' But instead he found himself exclaiming: 'Suffer the children to come unto me!' And with these words of the Saviour, he ended his sermon.

The congregation was left bewildered. The sermon had been short and rather muddled, confused, even. It had no kernel around which the ideas might coalesce.

The previous day, on Saturday evening, after he had returned from the bishopric, Father Ignatius had sent word to Hanna, via her husband Theodor Bistricki, whom he had bumped into on the street, that she should come to confession that Sunday without fail. This for three reasons: Firstly, never had she attended confession since she moved to the village. Secondly, perhaps she was being watched and it would be well for her to be seen at confession like any other good Christian. Thirdly, and most importantly: regardless of whether other people saw her or not, be they sinners or unblemished, the Lord Above saw all and knew all…

And so after the sermon, Theodor gently took Hanna by the arm and they both went before the priest. Father Ignatius waited for a few moments, but when he saw Hanna was silent and troubled, he asked her in a voice loud enough for all to hear: 'Do you wish to confess, Mrs Bistricki?'

Hanna nodded.

The priest sat down in the tall throne of gilded oak beneath its baldachin and drew the dark red curtain in front, but only halfway. Pale, her eyes feverish, Hanna knelt by the small window to the left of the chair, leaning her head on the lectern. She remained kneeling like that for a long time. The priest waited. Finally, he gently urged her: 'Speak, Mrs Bistricki! I am listening.'

Hanna remained silent.

'You'll see, it will be much easier for you afterward…'

Hanna was still silent.

'Confess your sins, that you may ease your soul!' said the priest, and without him wishing it, his voice betrayed a slight annoyance.

Hanna raised her head to the window and the priest became witness to the strangest, most upside-down confession he had ever heard.

In a whisper, Hanna said: 'I have not stolen!

'I have not killed!

'I have not lied or borne false witness!

'I have not coveted another's goods or envied another's happiness!

'I have not sinned in thought or deed before God or man!

'I have not blasphemed or gossiped or spoken ill of anybody!

'I have not done anybody harm!

'I have not wished anybody ill!

'I have not been faithless!

'I have not broken my word before God or man!

'Why then? Why then am I punished by God?'

She burst into tears, her body convulsed with sobs.

The priest was dumbfounded. He could not understand any of it. He had never heard such a confession before. It took a few moments before he came to his senses. Only then did he realise how reckless her words had been. He gave a frightened start and spoke quickly: 'It is a great sin for you, a mere mortal, to judge the actions of the Omniscient and Omnipotent. It is a grave sin for you to doubt

His justice. His hand alone holds the scales to weigh good and evil. What can we know? Go home, Mrs Bistricki, and pray! Pray hard and the Lord will forgive you…'

The end-of-the-month receptions given by Mr Pattunek the farm overseer and his beautiful dark-eyed wife, who wore her hair plaited like a crown around her head, continued untroubled by the war.

The Sunday-evening card games continued, too, with tea and rum and brandy for the men and sweet liqueurs for the ladies, held at the houses of now one, now another of the village notables, as if nothing had happened and nothing would happen in the world.

In attendance as always was the notary Thaddeus Andruschka, with his wooden leg, which, along with a medal for bravery, he had received in exchange for the real leg he had lost at Piave or Doberdo, nobody any longer knew where exactly. He would always be there, with his oak root walking stick, which he always kept to hand, hanging it from the back of his chair, with his gleaming bald patch, which seemed to have spread, and the tufts of ginger hair above his ears, which seemed to have shrunk. And as always, he was accompanied by Mrs Elvira Andruschka, as docile as ever, as admiring as ever of everything her husband said, as withered and tall as ever, with her wrinkled face and lovelocks of chestnut hair plastered to her forehead. Also in attendance were Dr Andrei Halinski, the director of the sanatorium, short, lively, with a sharp nose and serious mien, but whose seriousness slowly dissolved after the first glass of brandy, when the doctor would become merry, exuberant, garrulous, and Mrs Magdalena Halinski, the former nurse, sturdily built, barrel-chested, but gentle, with a small, round, childlike face, who sought to temper her husband, casting apologetic glances all around. Present too were agronomic engineer Theodor Bistricki and his wife Hanna. But instead of Mr Edvard Maturinski, the Sunday-afternoon tea parties were now attended by the new pharmacist, Mr Karl Rupert, a man of around forty, with bushy black eyebrows that shaded small eyes, sunken in their sockets. He was more taciturn, less elegant, and less polite and courteous toward the ladies than had been his predecessor, Mr Maturinski.

Karl Rupert had been given the 'Hypocrates' pharmacy to rent, furniture, medicaments, flacons and all. It was said that he had a wife and three children somewhere, but he had not brought his family to the village and never mentioned them. Rumours had sprung up around the tight-lipped pharmacist. Some said he was in the middle of a divorce, others that he had not even been married to the woman and the children were not his.

The men played cards, rummy, or poker, or sixty-six, or eight-nine, and the ladies either watched or discussed the latest fashions, the price of stockings, the weather, the war, a subject that had lately been added to their conversations and which prompted them to heave deep sighs: 'Oh! Will this war ever end?'

Hanna received the guests, served them their tea and drinks, answered their questions, but with complete apathy, her mind elsewhere or nowhere at all. But nobody noticed her absence while present, or her presence while absent, because each was wrapped up in himself or herself, each in fact spoke to himself or herself, liked to listen to his or her own voice, fervently wishing only that he or she might beat the others at cards.

The one who helped Hanna not to lose her mind, to keep hold of herself in the world, not to sink, was her husband Theodor. Hanna had grown very thin lately, her face was drawn, her eyes were misted and of a deeper blue, her hair was a darker blond, and when she loosened it in the evening, it seemed to fall to her shoulders more heavily. She had grown older. Suffering had made her more beautiful than ever and Theodor loved her insanely. He encouraged her, reassured her. The war would not last forever, the normal state of affairs was still peace, and those who had left or been forcibly taken away would come back home. And later, perhaps not long from now, they would look back on the present as a bad dream. Besides anything else, they were lucky that he had not yet been sent to the front. At the beginning of the war, Pattunek had straightaway arranged a mobilisation, but it seemed that he had overlooked Theodor since then…

Theodor kept her alive, afloat, he helped her not to sink, but it was something else that caused her to return among other people.

It was a Monday morning. Auntie Angela, the certified midwife, had come to visit her, she made her a cup of tea, she rummaged in search of sugar in the kitchen drawers, telling her all the latest news from the village. Hanna barely listened to her. Her mind barely registered anything. All of a sudden, a flush rushed to her cheeks and she felt a queasiness in her stomach. She leaned over the basin. Auntie Angela pressed a warm hand to Hanna's forehead and joyfully exclaimed: 'This is it!'

From that day hence, the midwife visited more often, to give advice, to keep an eye on things, and when the time came, Theodor did not have to pull on his trousers in the middle of the night and rush to fetch Auntie Angela, since she had set up shop the evening before and had everything ready when little Dora entered the world at three o'clock in the morning.

Dr Halinski was also present, out of friendship, out of caution, since after all it was the first time the young woman had given birth, but in effect he had had nothing to do. Auntie Angela had foreseen everything, arranged everything, done everything necessary.

All the while, Theodor had hoped and wished for a son. But when he saw the small, dark eyes blinking at the sudden light and heard the strong, healthy bawl released from the tiny chest, Theodor felt no regret. He fell in love with his daughter from the first instant. He asked that she be called Theodora, and Hanna, soaked in sweat, exhausted, still groggy from the throes of labour, nodded her assent. Soon the house was filled with diminutives spoken, called, sung in every tone of voice: Dora, Dorca, Dorica, Ica…

The little girl also brought something else new to their lives: the arrival of Theodor's parents.

His father, Marian Bistricki, a warm man with an open heart, and his mother, Marilena, who was colder, more distant, kissed the little girl, they kissed the new mother. They said nothing about the past. They spoke only of the baby, with Mrs Bistricki overwhelming her daughter-in-law with advice she did not need, since Auntie Angela had already given her it long before. Indeed, it was the qualified midwife herself who did most of the work, swaddling the baby, coming to bathe her…

After a few days, Theodor's parents went back home, reassured that all was going well and happy at having become grandparents.

With little Dora their house embarked upon a completely new life. They were more tired, they had more worries and cares, but also more satisfactions. Many a time Hanna and Theodor exchanged puzzled glances, as if wondering how they had lived up till then. Their life previous to the little girl's arrival seemed empty and meaningless to them. Their life now was washing nappies, it was sleepless nights spent wondering: Is there something wrong? What is it that hurts? The pain of her teething, the joy of her first syllables, which each parent was quick to interpret in his or her own way, with Hanna claiming the little one said 'Dada,' and Theodor that she clearly said 'Mama.'

One evening, in Dora's third year, by which time she followed her parents all around, clinging to her mother's skirts and asking endless questions, after they had put her to bed and sent her off to sleep with a long story about a king who had three sons – she did not fall asleep until the three princes had made their way in the world – Theodor remained sitting at the table, looking at Hanna in silence.

'Aren't we going to go to bed too, Theo?' Hanna asked, abashed by his silent gaze. 'Why are you looking at me like that?'

'I want to tell you something, Hanna. But you must promise me you won't get annoyed. And that you won't take it the wrong way…'

'Oho, how solemn you've become, Theo!' she laughed. 'All right, I promise whatever you like, but come on, out with it!'

'It's something serious, Hanna... I'm talking about the Friday-night candles...'

Hanna was left shocked and frightened. For a few seconds she was unable to say a word. Finally, she said in a soft voice: 'How did you know, Theo? Since when?'

'For a long time... from the very start. I found two candle stubs on the silver tray in the larder.'

'Then you know... You've known for years, but you said nothing?' And she was filled with a warm feeling of friendship. He was dear to her and she was proud of him for not having said anything to her about it for all those years, for not having tried to stop her, even for pretending that he did not know, so that she would not feel embarrassed.

'You know very well that I don't have any prejudices, Hanna. I go to church on Sunday because that's what people expect, the society we live in, especially in this small village, where everybody is looking at you. But I'd go to a synagogue or a mosque or a Buddhist temple just the same... Up till now, you've had to avoid the eyes of other people, on the outside, but now we have Dorica, our little girl... She asks questions about everything and goes everywhere in the house... including the larder,' said Theodor, with a smile. 'We'll never close any door to her, will we, Hanna?'

She nodded.

Theodor went on: 'If she sees the candles just once, and it's impossible for her not to see them sooner or later, she'll ask you questions and you'll have to answer. You'll have to tell her the truth... The plain, simple truth. Sabbath candles on Friday evening, and mass at church on Sunday... Why, Mama? Why don't other people do that? What then? She'll be in two minds all her life... two Gods, two faiths, two peoples. Without fully belonging to either, without genuinely believing in either... Why sow doubt in her soul by our own hand? Why give her all kinds of complexes? Why make her sail through life with each foot in a different boat? Isn't it better that we give her a healthy upbringing, within a single religion? I don't know how to explain it to you, Hanna…'

'There's no need for you to explain, Theo' she said softly and fell to thinking. A bitter smile flickered around her lips.

'What are you thinking?' he asked, feeling uneasy.

'We want every door to be open to her, at the price of some doors remaining locked forever.'

And before her eyes appeared her father, David Kamin the watchmaker, as he was on Saturday afternoons, with his round beard nicely trimmed, his face rested, now smooth as if by miracle, without a wrinkle, without a weekday care; she saw him bent over the thick old book bound in moth-eaten leather, searching it with his eyes. 'The love that depends on a thing perishes when that thing perishes. The love that does not depend on a thing will never perish,' she heard her father's warm murmur in her ears as he read, 'Be temperate and prudent… Do not be hasty to pass judgement… Judge every man for the best.' She saw the thin figure of her mother with the thick dog-eared book she had inherited from her mother and which her mother had inherited from her own mother and so on… where might that book be now, with its strange title, *Tzeena-Ureena*? Yes, 'let us go out, let us see'… from which her mother used to read to her those strange tales of long ago in a droning, singsong voice. Because of a cock and a hen carried at the head of a wedding procession, which greedy strangers had stolen, the City was destroyed… 'No, you're wrong, dear Theo, darling Theo!' she suddenly felt like shouting. 'Maybe we ought to tell her everything. Open to her every door, every window, every book… Even the ones we have never entered, looked inside, understood…' Because of a cart shaft the City was destroyed… The king's daughter ordered that a young firtree planted at the birth of a child be felled to make a shaft for her carriage… And because of an insult cast at a man in public, the City was destroyed… Because he was sent away from the table of the feast, driven out in shame, and none of the others seated at the table came to his defence… And so it was that in one part of the city there was feasting and merriment, while in the other part there was great slaughter. And those who feasted and made merry did not hear the cries of those cut down by the sword and pierced by the spear… In one part of the city flowed wine, in the other blood… And Hanna pictured her town, with its empty streets, her house, the door sealed by two red disks of wax and a piece of string, the clock repair shop, the old timepiece with the turrets on top and a white enamelled face around which were arranged elongated Roman numerals, the lanky man who had stood up from her father's workbench, the brickworks, the rusty gates hanging askew, the paths strewn with paper and rags, the empty huts and sheds, the silence, as if in a graveyard…

'I don't understand you… What doors are you talking about?' said Theodor softly, sensing she was far away, very far away.

Hanna smiled sadly: 'I understand you, Theo. I won't light those candles any more.'

Hanna kept her word. From that day hence, she no longer lit the Sabbath candles on Friday evening.

But for a long time, she lit them in her mind. She closed her eyes, covered them with her palms, and saw the candles vividly, burning with a frail flame, in tranquillity…

And behind the candles appeared the figure of her father, with his round chestnut beard, and the pale, wrinkled face of her mother. And behind them, the faces of her grandfather, with his long white beard, and her grandmother, wan and wrinkled, as she had once glimpsed them when she was very, very small. And behind them, the blurred faces of her great-grandfathers, with their even longer, even whiter beards, and her great-grandmothers, with their even thinner and even more wan faces, whom she had never seen, but whose presence she had sensed… An endless line of ancestors, fading into the white dust of time past… She gradually began to hear the ticking of the grand clock with its solid ebony case and its turrets, its white enamelled face and elongated Roman numerals… She could not see the hands, she heard only the calm, monotonous, heedless ticking…

Yes, time, arriving from some endless place, moved on. It moved on without pause, dragging Hanna behind it. Other days arrived, other events, the memories faded, and Hanna forgot the candles. She lit them neither in the larder nor anywhere else, not even in her mind. Caught up in the small, day-to-day things, she increasingly forgot what day it was. On Friday evening, she would forget that the next day was the Sabbath…

The end of the war brought a number of changes to the village. Of those who had been conscripted, a few returned, including seven with only one leg, three with only one arm, and one blind. Theodor looked in the mirror, felt his arms and legs, realising only then what a catastrophe he had escaped. At the beginning of the war, he had received an immediate mobilisation order at the farm, valid for one year, after which it would seem that they had forgotten about him, nor had he gone to make inquiry.

To Walnut Tree Lane, also known as Jews' Lane, nobody returned.

Karl Rupert, the taciturn pharmacist with the bushy eyebrows, who during the war had rented the 'Hypocrates' pharmacy, furniture, medicaments, flacons and all, asked for a transfer as soon as peace was declared and left the village overnight, without bidding anybody farewell. Auntie Angela, the certified midwife, who knew every secret and entered every door, and who often went to the pharmacy for supplies of rubbing alcohol and medicines, said that he had left out of embarrassment, lest the former owner return to find him comfortably at home in his pharmacy. But the former owner, Mr Evard Maturinski, did not return. A lady pharmacist from the sanatorium came to serve at the village pharmacy for a few hours every day.

Overseer Pattunek and his beautiful dark-eyed wife, who wore her plaited hair like a crown on top of her head, went away to foreign parts and never came back. Theodor Bistricki had to take over the running of the farm as a stopgap.

Notary Thaddeus Andruschka retired and, having rarely set foot in church and never having missed a card game, now he never missed a Sunday service, to the great satisfaction of his pious wife Elvira, and more and more seldom did they frequent the gatherings with tea and rum and brandy for the men and sweet liqueurs and gossip for the ladies. In any event, the gatherings themselves took place more and more seldom. On the other hand, Dr Halinski and Mrs Margareta and engineer Theodor Bistricki began increasingly to neglect churchgoing, perhaps because after the war there were greater numbers of pulmonary patients and a greater shortage of bread. Probably there was also a greater lack of religious faith, since many other people too, particularly the young, had begun to avoid the church, and Father Ignatius was alarmed to behold his ageing congregation. When an elderly parishioner departed for the next world, accompanied by the priest's hymns and prayers, his place in the pews would remain empty.

Although Theodor went to church more and more seldom because of his responsibilities at the farm, which had multiplied now he was the stopgap manager, Hanna still attended the services quite regularly. Not even she could explain to herself why. Perhaps it was out of inertia, or perhaps out of a vague, nebulous feeling of inferiority, since she knew in her heart of hearts that she had not been born into that community, or perhaps it was out of gratitude to the zealous priest who had saved her from the hands of that officer during the war and who now, in a deeply sorrowful voice, cried out his admonishments and promised forgiveness to those who did not regularly frequent the house of the Lord; he cried out, sometimes before the half-empty pews, but never within earshot of those at whom his words were aimed, those who were absent…

In particular, Hanna took care to submit to all the official rites to do with children. Theodora was baptised and then confirmed. The ceremonies made a big impression on the little girl: the white dress, the white flowers for a spotless little bride of Christ; they made her heart tremble with emotion. And so too did the silence beneath the high vaulted ceiling, the solemn hymns, the voice of the priest, which came as if from on high, from the azure sky painted with white angels, the head of the priest with his unruly hair combed back, who against the background of the yellow glow of the candles looked as if he were one of the gentle, suffering, haloed saints, having stepped down from the frescoed church wall. They all made a deep impression on the little girl.

The years passed and Theodor the young engineer became a mature, highly serious, respectable man. He had put on a little weight, his chestnut hair had greyed at the temples, which suited him well, and he had become the father of two children. For in the meantime, when Theodora was seven, her sister, Eva-Magdalena, was born. Her parents called her Evuni. Auntie Angela, the qualified midwife, was more wrinkled than she had been seven years earlier, when Theodora was born, but she was just as skilled, just as lively and talkative. Dr Halinski was also present at the birth, and was just as unneeded as the first time. Theodor was slightly disappointed: he had been expecting a boy even more confidently than he had the first time, but he resigned himself just as quickly as after the arrival of his first daughter.

Theodor's parents arrived in a hurry to see their new granddaughter. They kissed the baby, they kissed the mother and the elder daughter. Mrs Bistricki, distinguished and a little distrait, overwhelmed her daughter-in-law with advice, which Hanna did not need, since she had already received it from Auntie Angela, and anyway she now knew it from experience, after her first child. And a few days later, Theodor's parents left. The whole family now spent their holidays at Theodor's parents'. Hanna felt awkward in that large house with its air of foreignness, but she did not say anything to anybody. In the house of her parents-in-law she spoke little and never contradicted Mrs Marilena Bistricki. When she was alone with her husband, Theodor's mother was moved to observe that even if she had become part of their family against her will, at least she was a good and obedient daughter-in-law…

The years passed, Theodor's temples greyed, but it suited him. Once, when he came home from work, he caught Hanna combing her hair in the mirror and seeking to conceal some white strands. Silver strands that had appeared just above her forehead. Hanna was taking great pains to conceal them under a lock of her dark blond hair.

When she saw him loom suddenly in the mirror, Hanna gave a start.

'There's no need, Hanni,' Theodor said with a smile. 'It's nicer like that…'

And he kissed her gently on the top of her head.

One day, Theodora, the eldest girl, and a few of her friends from school were playing in the garden. It was a beautiful, warm spring day. The sky was serene, and the rolling green hills showed limpidly, dotted by blossoming fruit trees, like bouquets of pink and white flowers.

Hanna was sitting on the terrace, darning some socks; Dora tore holes in her socks so often it was beyond belief. Theo wanted a boy, and he had one, in the form of his eldest daughter. She was her father's little girl. Theodor and Dorca got on together wonderfully well. The father forgave all his daughter's mischief. He was even proud of it: the fences she leaped, the trees she climbed, the scratches on her nose, the stones she threw, missing their target and breaking the windows of their house or the neighbours'… Little Evuni was completely different: timid, gentle, obedient. She followed her elder sister everywhere, in silent admiration, trying to imitate her, but without much success…

From time to time, Hanna cast a glance at the playing girls, smiling at a memory. The games had been the same in her day:

hopscotch, ball, skipping rope, tag, hide-and-seek… Had children played like that a hundred years ago? A thousand years ago? But even so, how new those games were to them now, how fresh… Perhaps because they too were new, and only they were able to live in the present so serenely, so fully, without caring what had happened yesterday, without fearing what would happen tomorrow…

All of a sudden Evuni found herself getting in the way of the older girls.

'Go and sit over there! You're in the way,' shouted Dora and taking her by the shoulders, she led her to the terrace and made her sit on the bottom step.

The girls played, shouted, all of them talking all at once, making such a commotion that it was impossible to hear anything anyone was saying. It was then that Hanna heard her daughter shout: 'Quiet, girls! Don't talk all at once like you were in a synagogue!'

Hanna gave a start. She immediately called her back inside.

'Dorca, where did you hear those words, 'like in a synagogue'?'

'From Vladi,' answered the girl, surprised at her mother's anger. Vladi was the nephew of the notary Andruschka and he visited his uncle in the holidays. He was a student, studying pharmaceutics in his first year. Uncle Thaddeus Andruschka and Aunt Elvira had plans for him to become the village pharmacist, and they also saw themselves becoming in-laws of the Bistricki family… Vladimir and Dora got on very well together; they spent the whole holiday going for walks…

'Vladi says that at the synagogue everybody prays all at once, shouting over the top of each other like savages, and they all have big beards and side-whiskers, and all they do is make business deals.'

'That's not true! They're just like everybody else and it's not nice to make fun of other peoples and other religions… Especially when you don't know anything, when you haven't the slightest idea…'

She thought of the synagogue on the main street, on the corner with Walnut Tree Lane, which was now empty, its doors hanging askew, its windows broken, and she would have liked to tell the girl that her grandfather had worn a beard, that he was a watchmaker, that he went to the synagogue and prayed in a loud voice when he was in pain… But she did not tell her any of this, only: 'Go back outside, Dorca, play with the girls.'

Engineer Theodor Bistricki was busier and busier. Previously, the tonnes of cereals, fruit, milk, meat had been goods, expressed in figures: price, revenue, profitability, bourse index. But now, after the war, they had gone back to being what they were at the beginning of time: food. Food that had to be shared among all, so that nobody would suffer want, nobody would be humiliated… In those times, after the war, the urge to work was like an unstoppable flood, it drove gearwheels, unleashing unimagined energies in the natural world and in people's hope-filled hearts and minds.

As the days and weeks passed, the farm became a large enterprise, carrying out research into the climatic adaptation of new varieties of cereal. Engineer Bistricki, thitherto the stopgap manager, was appointed director of the farm.

There was a lot of work to do, what with mechanisation, the different crops, and, above all the workers. There were all kinds: young and inexperienced, peasants with long experience, much of it out of date, and who sometimes had trouble understanding the new methods. Theodor had a lot of headaches because of the new laboratory and above all because of the laboratory assistant, a young woman who added white hairs to the ones he already had on his temples.

Recently having graduated with a degree in industrial chemistry, she turned up at his office one Saturday. With her boyishly short brown hair, her overly broad face and jaw, and her snub nose, she was not beautiful, but she had very light-coloured eyes, which looked now green, now blue, depending on how they caught the light. The farm's director looked her up and down. She was wearing a blue dress with a white collar, visible beneath her unbuttoned light grey raincoat, and on her head, she wore a blue beret. She gave the impression of being unassuming, tidy, serious. But how to tell with young people nowadays? You can never judge from a first impression. The girl entered and stood timidly by the door.

'Come in, come in! Take a seat!' Bistricki encouraged her.

The girl came closer, rummaged in her handbag, handed him the official document stating that Veronica Andrea Baran, chemist, had been assigned to the farm as a laboratory assistant.

'Look here, it's Saturday today,' said director Bistricki, in an official tone of voice, perfunctory but at the same time friendly, 'you must be tired after the journey, go and have a rest. Tomorrow, you'll come and have Sunday lunch at my house, and on Monday morning, at seven o'clock, you'll start work. All right?'

'Thank you.'

'Do you have somewhere to stay?'

'No. I've just arrived. My suitcase is outside, in the antechamber.'

'I'll have somebody help you find good lodgings.'

'Thank you, director!'

On Sunday, Veronica Baran came to lunch. Hanna took a liking to her from the very first moment. What with her broad jaw and snub nose, Hanna thought her plain, but likeable. After the meal, Veronica insisted on playing ball with the girls.

As she was leaving, Hanna said to her: 'Come every Sunday, Veronica… Come whenever you like.'

'Thank you!'

But at seven o'clock on Monday, the new chemist did not arrive for work. She had still not arrived by nine and then ten o'clock. Angry at first, Theodor grew worried. He sent somebody to the room she rented, in a house at the end of Ram's Lane, below the hill, but she was not there; nor had she spent the night there. It was not until eleven o'clock that she arrived for work, wearing short trousers without stockings, red sandals tied with ribbons at the ankle, a blue blouse, and a red headscarf. She was covered in dust from head to toe.

'Please forgive me, director,' she mumbled, out of breath, 'I hurried to get here –'

'So I see,' said the director, ironically.

'Yesterday, I went to my uncle's in town and my cousin gave me a lift back this morning on his motorbike, so that I would be here at seven, but it broke down –'

'Is this any way to dress for work?'

'I'm very sorry, but I didn't want to be even later than I was already.'

'Well then, go home, miss, get changed, and come straight back to work, since there are quite a few things need doing around here…'

At dinner, Theodor told Hanna what had happened. She laughed: 'What do you expect? She's young.'

'I was young too, once,' said Theodor, annoyed, 'but I knew the meaning of responsibility from the very start. I would never have dared to show up three hours late on my first day, to present myself in front of overseer Pattunek wearing short trousers…'

Some time after that, Theodor complained to his wife: 'That girl doesn't know much about chemistry. God knows how she got a degree. I have to waste hours at a time in the laboratory, showing her how to conduct tests…'

'Have a little patience, Theo! She's still young. She doesn't have the practical experience yet.'

'And do you think she was late only on her first day? She's reliably late. Every morning. And every morning her supposed cousin gives her a lift on his motorbike… I'd be very interested to see what kind of a cousin he is…'

'In the end, is it any of your business, Theo?' asked Hanna in amazement.

'You're right. What business is it of mine?'

It was Monday morning, and Theodor Bistricki, the farm's director, strode angrily from the administrative offices to the laboratory and back. He had done so dozens of times already. It was eight o'clock and she still hadn't arrived. She was always half an hour late, sometimes more than an hour late. And she had work to do: he had given her some grain samples to test. The tests were very important, and urgent too. How could young people be so blasé? Today, he was going to tell her straight out: 'Miss, either you want to work or you don't. But tell me which it is to be, so that I know whom I can rely on! If the answer is yes, then arrive at work on time. We have urgent work to do. The ministry is asking for results. If the answer is no, then you still need to tell me because then… then I can take measures… No, don't be afraid miss! I'm not going to give you the sack, even though that's what you deserve, to be booted out… If you don't want to do your work, then stay at home, or go for motorcycle rides with that supposed cousin of yours, go wherever you like with him, and I'll have the driver bring your wages to you at home in a sealed envelope… just don't let me set eyes on you around here again!'

Berating her in his mind, he entered his office. On his desk he saw two white wildflowers, crossed like swords. He looked up and saw Veronica Baran standing aside. She was wearing a flowery summer dress, on top of which she had quickly pulled her white lab coat. His anger subsided as if by miracle. He looked at the crossed flowers in front of him.

'Director, please forgive me but –'

'I know,' interrupted Bistricki, 'you came by motorcycle and so on and so forth –'

'No, I didn't go anywhere. Last night, I didn't feel well, and this morning I slept in…'

She slept in! Good God, what a poor excuse! Unbelievable! The girl has some cheek, that's for sure… If he had tried to fob off Mr Pattunek with an excuse like that… He didn't know whether to laugh or cry. But his gaze fell on the white flowers, so small and so delicate, lying crossed on the table, as if winking at him.

Calmly, almost in a good mood, he said, 'There's a lot of work to do, Miss Veronica.'

A few hours later, after he had visited the crops section, after he had spoken to the mechanics in the repairs shop and given them their instructions, he went to the laboratory. For a time, without saying anything, he watched her work. Veronica did not notice him enter, or else she pretended not to notice… Over her broad face played rays of sunlight, refracted through the glass of the test tubes and alembics, flickering in every colour of the spectrum, and in her very light-coloured eyes glinted strange hues, making one seem azure, the other pale green, as she frowned in concentration. Theodor felt like smiling at the childlike concentration and seriousness with which she performed her task with the test tube.

In an off-hand, slightly joking way, he asked her: 'That young man who takes you for motorbike rides on Sundays, is he really your cousin?'

Without intending to, he had adopted a paternal, protective tone of voice.

She turned her gaze from the test tube and looked at him in surprise.

'What business is it of yours, director? Does it have anything to do with the laboratory?'

A trace of irony could be detected in her voice.

Bistricki recalled that he had been asked the same question before.

'Oh, no, not at all! It's none of my business!'

'In that case, I can answer your question: he really is my cousin, my genuine cousin, on my mother's side. His mother and mine are sisters, in other words…' She paused and then continued, gloomily: 'I imagine that in this dead-end village, there must be all kinds of rumours about me…'

'I haven't heard any so far. Anyway, I couldn't care less about what the village is saying, or the town, or the country, or the whole world… I don't harbour prejudices of any kind whatever,' said Bistricki, not without a certain hint of pride, and taking a bottle off a shelf he handed it to her, saying: 'Add a little acid, it has to react…'

And then he went to his office, where he had a great deal of work to do: reports and letters to write, supplies to order, instructions to issue.

Veronica came back to work after lunch. There was urgent work to do, and by late that evening, all the bottles with test samples had been sealed with wax, the analysis sheets had been filled in, and the parcels had been made up, ready for the director to give the order for them to be posted to the Institute of Agronomic Research and the ministry the next morning.

Bistricki looked at the clock.

'It's eleven p.m., Miss Veronica! If you had started earlier in the morning, you would have finished long ago.'

'Yes, I know, director. It won't happen again.

'Not until next Monday? Or not until tomorrow?' asked the director, as she removed her lab coat, quickly adding: 'I can't let you walk home alone at this time of night. I'll take you. It's a long way to the end of Ram's Lane. And it's pitch black…'

'Oh, I'm not afraid!' protested Veronica, without great conviction.

Outside, the coachman had the light one-horse trap ready.

'Go home to bed, Mihai,' Theodor told the old man. 'I'll drive the trap.'

The old man went off, mumbling 'goodnight, sir,' and thinking to himself that the director might have told him earlier instead of making him wait till that hour.

Bistricki helped the girl climb into the trap and then went around the other side, jumped aboard, sat down next to her, and took the reins. The horse slowly walked down the dark road that led away from the farm offices and then turned onto the main road, which was dimly lit by yellow electric bulbs burning high up on the widely spaced telegraph poles. Finally, they turned down Ram's Lane. Here the darkness was absolute, with not one star in the sky, not one light on earth. The black outlines of the silent houses on either side of the lane were barely visible. The road was in poor repair, potholed and strewn with stones. Whenever the light trap gave a jolt, Theodor felt the girl's shoulder touch his.

He moved closer…

'We're here!' she said suddenly.

They had reached the end of the lane, at the bottom of the hill.

'This is where I live,' she said and fell silent.

The only sound was the monotonous purling of the stream at the back of the garden.

He waited for a little while and then said: 'Aren't you going to invite me inside? To tell you the truth, I ought to have come long ago, to check on the farmworkers' lodgings…'

'It's very late…' she mumbled, undecided.

'Another time, then. Good night.'

'Good night.'

She entered the house.

Had he insisted, I would have invited him inside, thought Veronica, after she lit the lamp. It was so depressing to live alone in a rented room like that… one bed, one table, two chairs, an old cupboard, eaten away by woodworms… It would have been interesting to see how a stern, proud director like him would have looked in my room… But it's better this way… There's no point…

I was as shy and stupid as a schoolboy, thought Theodor, holding the reins loosely as he made his way home. Had I insisted, she would have invited me inside. I shouldn't even have asked her, I should have just taken her by the arm and led her inside… No matter, another time… another time… another time… murmured Theodor to the rhythm of the wheels of the trap… Or maybe never… What would be the point? What business have I in that room? Another time, never… Another time, never… Another time, never…

He abruptly tugged on the reins. The trap came to a stop in front of his house. The light was on in the dining room; Hanna was waiting for him with his dinner on the table.

That was what she always did. No matter how late he came home, he always found a meal waiting, with her sitting at the table, holding needlework at which she wasn't working or a book she wasn't reading. It had started to annoy him. Why did she need to guard his dinner like an Alsatian? And then there were her irritating questions: 'Did you have a lot of work to do today? Are you tired? Weren't you hungry? If you can't come home earlier, I could bring your dinner to the office.' That would be all he needed… In the end, she could just as well put his dinner on the table and go to bed. Or else he could fetch the food from the kitchen himself. Why did she need to sit up waiting for him?

Auntie Angela the certified midwife, her face more wrinkled than ever, curls of unruly yellow hair poking from beneath her once dark brown headscarf, now faded thanks to soap and sunlight, lively, energetic, garrulous Auntie Angela used to visit Hanna from time to time, to see the girls she had brought into the world and whose nappies she had changed when they were little. The fact was that she regarded as her own all the children from the village and surrounding area, she knew what had become of all of them, whether they had had measles, chickenpox or whooping cough, what marks they got at school, what they liked to eat, everything about them. Little Evuni was the dearest to her. Theodora was now almost a young lady, who no longer let herself be patted on the cheek. You could no longer tell her fairy tales about the stork delivering new-born babies down the sooty chimney… But little Evuni listened to Auntie Angela's long and rather convoluted stories about fairies and dragons and birds of ill omen, gazing at her with her wide-open blue eyes. The old woman liked to sit with the little girl when she did her schoolwork, to watch her as she carefully traced straight lines, sloping lines, loops, which, as if by miracle, formed letters and then words: A… n… a, Ana, m… a… m… a, mama…

When the children were not at home, Auntie Angela, in accordance with her old habit, used to follow Hanna around the house. She would follow her into the kitchen. She did not sit still for one moment, like a guest waiting to be regaled, but went to help Hanna, she would fetch the salt and pepper for her, open this box, close that box, dry a saucer, put it on the shelf. She knew where everything was and where everything should go, she knew as well as the mistress of the house herself. And all the while she would recount everything that had happened in the village and round about, who had fallen out with whom, who had done whom a bad turn, who had spoken ill of whom, except that she herself did not believe it… She merely recounted what she had heard, but she herself refused to think ill of anybody…

On one of those beautiful, sunny spring mornings, when Theodor was at work and the children were at school, Auntie Angela entered the kitchen, more wrinkled than ever, her hair curlier and unrulier than ever, to make herself a cup of tea. She rummaged in a box looking for the sugar, sat down on a stool, and remained completely silent.

Hanna looked at her in amazement for a while. Then she grew intrigued.

'Is there anything wrong, Auntie Angela? Why the downcast face? Aren't you feeling well? Or hasn't anything worth telling happened in the village? Hasn't anything happened even in the outlying villages?'

'Yes, something has happened, and that's the problem… I came to talk to you, my girl… You see, in the village, folk have started talking about… about your husband… about how he's been spending too much time with that girl… in the laboratory… in other words, about how he's been seeing her…'

Hanna listened and the vague fear she herself had sensed up till then began to take on a firm outline. She too had suspected something. Major changes had come over Theodor lately. He had been coming home late, he was distrait, preoccupied, irritable. She had put it down to his stressful job, the great responsibilities that weighed on his shoulders as director of the farm. But she realised that it was not that. In any case, it was not only that... And now here was Auntie Angela, telling her... without adding, 'but I don't believe a word of it myself.' It would seem that even she had come to believe something...

After a long moment, Hanna burst into loud, strained laughter: 'You are the one telling me this, Auntie Angela? Don't you know how people in the village gossip? My husband tells me everything... The girl is young, she's still inexperienced, and Theodor has to show her how to do the job...'

'But they say he goes to her house, at night,' said the old woman in a faint voice. 'You need to have a talk with him. A man of his age, the closer it gets to closing time, as they say, if he loses his head, he'll start acting like a child... You need to talk to him, quietly, nicely, without quarrelling... So that he won't forget his family... Two young girls... A thing like that doesn't sit well.'

'Don't worry, Auntie Angela, don't get upset,' said Hanna, her heart thudding, 'it won't be anything at all! But even if it's something,' she added quickly. 'But I don't think it's anything. Probably he cares about the girl because she's hardworking, clever, he helps her and people started talking... But it isn't anything... Don't worry yourself for nothing.'

And Hanna tried to smile.

'Let's hope to God it isn't, my girl, let's hope to God...'

'Did you have a lot of work today?'
Of course he had a lot of work.
'Are you tired?'
Of course he's tired. Those niggling questions irritated the life out of him. Why doesn't she ask him something else? She obviously knows. She must know. Everybody knows. Dr Halitski answered him coolly whenever he said hello to him. Andruschka the notary and his tall scrawny wife with the curls plastered to her forehead barely answered his greeting at all and did not stop to talk. They were in

a hurry. They were always in a hurry when he met them on the street, although what urgent business could a pensioner like Andruschka and his wife have… And they no longer came to visit on Sunday afternoons. What prejudice-ridden people! What a hive of gossip that village was! They all weighed you up, judged you, condemned you. Without trial. Without any right to appeal! The only people who ought to have the right to judge love and people in love ought to be lovers… the only ones who can understand… Theodor almost burst out laughing: Would that mean that only thieves and burglars should judge robbers and housebreakers? How absurd? Lovers should never be judged by anybody! They should be understood…

But why didn't Hanna ask him anything? Why didn't she quarrel with him? It would have been easier for him. He would have tried to understand. But she kept her silence.

'Did you have a lot of work today?'
'Are you tired, Theo?'
That was all she said, and every night she waited for him with the table laid. The silence ground away at his nerves. There was a tension in the house, which kept growing. With each passing day, it grew more and more unbearable, like a boiler under pressure, with no release valve. In the house, it was unbearable; outside, it was hostile. Only in the garden of the little house at the end of Ram's Lane did he feel a different man. Lying in the grass at the bottom of the garden, at the foot of the hill, by the brook, which purled melodiously, monotonously, gazing at the supple green blades of grass, the trunks of the apple trees, the blue sky and rolling white clouds through the foliage, he felt happy. He was busy all day in the fields, but didn't see the grass; he saw tonnes of apples loaded in railcars, but he didn't see the apple tree with its fine-veined leaves and its fruit as it began to turn red, as if blushing bashfully; he saw the weather, be it overcast, raining or sunny, but he didn't see the blue sky and the white clouds.

There in the garden at the end of Ram's Lane, at the foot of the hill, by the crystal brook, it was heaven on earth. A genuine paradise, with soft green grass, the apple tree heavy with fruit, and next to him the warm young body of Veronica, wrapped in a soft dressing gown after she had bathed in the pure water of the stream. It was paradise, whereas on the other side of the fence were the village, people, a village full of prejudices, which talked about you, weighed you up, judged you, condemned you. Without trial. Without the right to appeal. Without listening to you or trying to understand you. There was not one person without prejudices. You could expect it of Thaddeus Andruschka the notary and his wife and Auntie Angela, who looked at him as if he had killed his own grandmother. But what about a man like Dr Andrei Halinski, who had married out of love, taking for his wife a humble nurse, setting his whole family against him? Even a man like him had rigid, hidebound ideas and now could no longer understand.

And at home, a wife who knew – she could hardly not know – and who pretended she didn't know, so that nothing would change in that dreary, monotonous life of theirs, God forbid! She was capable of closing her eyes, conforming to the village, to society, living a lie, all to keep things as they were.

But who knows? Maybe she really didn't have any knowledge of what was happening around her? Busy with the girls, with the petty everyday concerns of housekeeping, washing, darning, shopping, cooking, it was possible that she had not noticed anything, not heard anything, not found out anything. But nevertheless, she would have to find out. Nor could the situation with Veronica Baran be allowed to go on like that interminably. She was a young girl and she was in the firing line of all the village gossip, prejudice and nasty looks.

Or maybe Theodor was wrong and all of it – Veronica and the laboratory, the little room in the house at the end of Ram's Lane, at the foot of the hill, that corner of paradise with green grass and a murmuring brook and the blue sky and the white, enchanting body of the young woman to whom he felt attracted – all of it was just a momentary lapse, the warm, pleasant, heart-melting dream of a fleeting moment, but which seemed long, endlessly long, as long as a lifetime, and from which he would awake at any moment, banging his head against the wall, to find the same grey, enervating everyday reality as before: 'Are you tired, Theo? Maybe you're hungry?'

Hanna had suspected something even before, but after she talked to Auntie Angela, who had not concluded with her usual, 'But I don't believe it myself,' she now knew more, albeit not everything, or else she did not dare to think too far ahead. There were hours and minutes when she even hoped that none of it was true. Or that it was just a passing infatuation that would soon fizzle out, after which everything would go back to normal. But she didn't ask him any question. Perhaps she was waiting for Theodor to broach the subject? Or did she hope that he wouldn't broach it? What would have been the point of words, explanations, excuses, accusations anyway? Did she hope that it would all pass without leaving a trace, like a bad dream, a nightmare?

One fine day, Theodor would come home early, in a good mood, he would stroke her hair the way he used to, and say: 'No, Hanna! Leave that lock of silver hair alone. Don't hide it. It's nicer the way it is.'

She would clasp his hands. She would bury her face in his warm palms.

What mad dreams, mad, mad…

But why mad? They had a house, two daughters…

'Are you tired, Theo? Did have a lot of work today?'

She didn't have the courage to ask him other questions. She was afraid of the answer.

'Enough!' yelled Theodor one evening, sitting at the table, face to face with Hanna, who as ever had been waiting for him with his dinner ready. 'Don't you think it's time we had a serious talk, Hanna?'

'Yes, I do,' she said curtly.

'We've always been honest with each other.'

'We used to be,' she said softly.

'We've never hidden anything,' Theodor went on, still avoiding the subject at hand.

'We didn't used to!'

'But now we've ended up hiding from each other!'

'I haven't, Theodor,' said Hanna sadly, but firmly.

Theodor lost his temper: 'Can't you see the way we've been living together lately?'

'No, Theodor, we both eat, go to bed, breathe, move around under the same roof, but we don't live together.'

'As if that was what this is all about! You know me, you know I can't stand lies, and I'm not prepared to make compromises for the sake of society. And you're the same, Hanna! Neither of us was prepared to do that when we first met. Do you remember? Our families and everybody else were against us, but we stayed true to ourselves. Do you think it's easy for me to tell you now… but you can see it for yourself, Hanna, we have to separate.'

She made no answer. The silence between them deepened. Had things come to this? She had been afraid of it all the while, but she hadn't believed it would really happen. But now she had heard it with her own ears. She had heard it all too well.

'If only things were so simple, but they're not, Theodor,' she murmured, hopelessly.

'Because we go out of our way to make them complicated!' he yelled angrily. 'We won't be the first, and we won't be the last.'

'I know what I owe you, Theodor,' Hanna went on, in a quiet voice. 'You saved my life and you gave me a home. But if now you are taking that home away from me, what need of that life do I have any longer? You should have let me go with my parents.'

Theodor was left surprised; he hadn't been expecting such words. He was about to say something, but she went on: 'But even so, if I were the only one it affected… I know you don't have any prejudices or superstitions' – a trace of irony now crept into her voice – 'I know you are very frank, and that's nice, Theodor. If it were only the two of us, then people, society… but there are also the children. We have two daughters, Theodor! Wake up! Sometimes I get the feeling that I'm having a bad dream. That none of it is real… But we have to wake up, Theodor! Our girls need you and me, regardless of whether we still love each other or not.'

'But I have no intention of abandoning them! They'll have us both, they'll have me and they'll have you, Hanna!'

'They need a home, not a ruin!' she said, raising her voice. 'How can you be so naïve? This is also about you, and don't be angry at me for saying it so directly. Maybe you've forgotten. Maybe you don't realise, but you're not as young as you were. You're almost twice her age. She's a young woman, maybe an affair like this is interesting for her now, you're a mature man, you're experienced, you're greying at the temples, but what about in five years' time, in ten years' time, in fifteen years' time?'

'I see you're very considerate, you think of everybody: yourself, the children, me!' he said, feeling the blow to his self-love. 'But there's one person you haven't thought of in your self-centredness, Hanna, and that's Veronica Andrea Baran. You can mock her feelings in front of me, I can overlook that, but think about the situation she's in.'

'She ought to have thought of it herself before it all started!'

'You don't know her and you have no right to judge her! She's not just any other girl. She comes from a good family, she's educated, she studied at university…'

Hanna was stunned. The words 'good family,' 'educated,' 'studied at university,' 'good family,' 'educated,' went around and around in her mind. What was it supposed to mean?

'You have to understand, Hanna, that now you know everything, now you know about Veronica and me, we can't carry on like this, as if nothing had happened.'

Hanna remained silent.

'Haven't you a single ounce of pride, woman?' said Theodor rancorously.

'Pride'? The word became to spin around and around in her mind like a paper windmill. She had a family. Two children. Two girls. That was her pride. That was her only fulcrum in space and time: her family. Her husband, the children. Without them she would be borne away on the furious waves and quickly sink to the bottom, no matter how hard she thrashed her arms and legs.

No, no! No pride! What was happening to Theodor would pass. It was a passing blindness, a passion, powerful perhaps, but it would pass, like a storm. He would then realise that it wasn't for him, that at his age it wasn't possible to live like that, he would come to his senses, he would come back to her and his daughters.

Pride? No, it had no meaning. In the end, what was pride? A word. An inflated word, hollow inside. The storm would pass and tranquillity would return to their lives. She had been through so many things. With Theodor she had been through so many things. Her daughters needed a home in which to live, to grow, to learn, a place from which to set out in life and then make their own homes.

'We have to divorce, Hanna!'

'No! Never!'

She quickly ran to the children's room so that nobody would see the tears she could not hold back.

The children were asleep. Hanna wept softly, so as not to wake them.

From that evening forward, you could talk to Hanna about anything at all, about the weather, the children, the house, fashion, politics, anything except divorce. When Theodor brought up the subject of divorce, he would come up against the invariable response: 'No! It's never going to happen!'

It was like a concrete wall. Grey, impenetrable.

'No! Never!'

Weeks and months passed. A summer, an autumn, a winter passed, a new spring arrived. There seemed no way out of the situation. Theodor suggested that he leave home and move in with Veronica, in the cottage at the end of Ram's Lane. He would then be able to file for divorce on the grounds of having abandoned the conjugal home. But the girl was having none of it.

'You can't move in with me, Theo, not unless you get a divorce first, not unless we get married. Maybe until then you oughtn't to visit me at all.'

'Is that what you want, Veronica?'

'What about you, Theo? Would you be able to stop coming?'

Such tender, childlike questions often arose during their most earnest discussions. Questions answered with another question. 'Would you be able to live without me?' 'Would you?' 'Would you be able not to think about me any more?' 'Would you?'

In her lodgings, in her little room dimly lit by a lamp with a pink shade, Veronica gently released herself from his embrace and continued, in annoyance: 'You always forget the situation I'm in, Theo, dear, the way people see me here in the village… the way my parents would see me at home, if they knew. It doesn't even bear thinking about. They're old-fashioned, filled with pride, a sense of honour, prejudices. And I'm their only daughter. Their sole treasure. Understand? I'm the only daughter of lawyer Andrei Baran. Society, the law, marital status, and all the other trifling things that for him are life itself…'

'Yes, that's all very well,' blurted Theodor, in exasperation, 'but can't you see that we're going around and around in a vicious circle, with no way out? Doesn't it make your mind reel? I mean to say, I can't come here and stay with you without a divorce, and I can't get a divorce unless I leave home and come here…'

'And if you leave home, who will file for divorce? You? You'll go to court and say, "I've left home, please give me a divorce?" Don't you see that she's still the one who has to file for it? We need to have her consent!'

'Ah, yes, it's obvious from a mile away that you're a lawyer's daughter,' said Theodor, with irony in his voice.

But Veronica could not be more serious: 'Understand, Theo, that it's better for me, too. We're not in the jungle and I'm not a savage to snatch you away from her like that. She's a decent woman, who has given you children and the best years of her life. We can only be together if she consents to a divorce.'

'But what if she won't hear of it? I've even spoken to her harshly, but she merely listens in silence. And all she'll say is, "No, never!" She won't budge one inch. She's so devilishly stubborn!'

'She'll agree to it. You need to be patient. Talk to her and in the end, you'll find the right word to persuade her.'

Veronica Andrea Balan could not have suspected how prophetically she had just spoken. Very soon, without him even trying, Theodor was to find the word that would persuade her.

Theodor Bistricki was tired, vexed, exasperated, torn between two lives.

One Friday, as Hanna was serving him his lunch, Theodor sat eating, his eyes fixed on his plate. The two girls looked now at one parent, now at the other. By now, Theodora was sixteen, a tall, svelte, dark-eyed girl. Eva-Magdalena was nine; she had her mother's blue eyes and her father's dark chestnut hair. Two pairs of eyes rested now on one parent, now on the other. Dorca's dark, inquisitive eyes, Evuni's clear blue, frightened eyes.

'Daddy, why don't you talk to Mama? Why do you just eat without saying a word?' asked Theodora. She cared deeply about her father.

'Because I don't have anything to say,' he answered, in embarrassment, casting an angry glance at Hanna.

'Go to your room and do your schoolwork!' said Hanna and began to clear the table.

After the children had gone out, Theodor yelled at her furiously: 'You've even turned the girls against me! Very nice!'

'I haven't turned anybody against you. They have eyes to see!'

'To see what? There wouldn't be anything to see unless you showed them! They wouldn't hear anything unless you filled their heads with all kinds of nonsense. You use them to keep me tethered to you like an ox to a cart my whole life, you and your Jewish obstinacy!'

Theodor abruptly fell silent, astonished at himself. It was as if he had just heard another man's voice, a voice that was nonetheless his own. But how? Where did it come from? From what dark depths had the word erupted? Might some filthy clot have been lurking unknown deep inside him, obscured beneath layers of reading and education, beneath liberal feelings of humanity and love, only now to be raked up by blind rage, causing the reproach to erupt like lava, without him being able to predict it or stop it? Theodor was left dumbstruck, helpless, not knowing what to do. The word had rung out and could not be sucked back inside from the air through which it had now spread.

Hanna stood rigid, her face as white as chalk. But only for a few moments. In a faint but determined voice she then said: 'You are right, Theodor, we have to separate.'

The questions that had tortured her for so many months: What would become of the children? What would become of her? Where would she go, at her age? now suddenly seemed completely meaningless. There was now an answer to all of them, the only possible answer: 'We have to separate, Theodor.'

It was all so simple.

Theodor left the house, slamming the door behind him in a fury. He was furious at himself.

Hanna gave a start. She remembered the children. Might they have heard something? She had to be with them. She went to the girls' room. It was empty. Their schoolbooks were scattered over the table.

Hanna went outside and called for them. No answer. She went to look for them at the neighbours' houses. She started at the houses next door. She then went to the houses of Theodora's friends, Evuni's friends. The girls were nowhere to be found. Nobody had seen them. She went to the house of Andruschka the notary, nobody there. Auntie Angela was not at home. As usual, her door was unlocked. Almost at a run, she went to Dr Halinski's sanatorium, three kilometres away. The girls had not been there. She did not know where they could have gone. A deathly fear gripped her.

Maybe in the meantime they had gone home and she would find them at the table doing their schoolwork. She was running back from the sanatorium when behind her she heard the rumble of an engine. Dr Halinski had sent the hospital car to take her home.

She went inside the house. All the rooms were empty. Her legs were trembling. She sat down at the children's table, looked at the schoolbooks scattered over it, her mind incapable of thought. Dusk was falling. Dark shadows crept through the room. A thought now flashed through her mind: It was Friday. Friday evening. She quickly got up and went to the larder, where she lit two candles on the silver tray. She covered her eyes with her palms. She moved her lips soundlessly. She had long ago forgotten the prayer. She stood for a long time. Heavy, salty teardrops trickled through her fingers, more and more teardrops.

The girls had indeed heard everything. Theodora, pale, her dark eyes flashing, her lips clenched tight so that she would not burst into tears, took her younger sister's hand and said: 'Let's go, Evuni!'

'Where are we going, Dorca?' asked the little girl, frightened.

Without answering, Dorca dragged her off behind her. They ran into the street and went up the main road to the church. They went to the bottom of the churchyard, where there was a small house, whose walls the priest had painted ultramarine. Hanna would never have thought to look for the girls there…

Theodora knocked on the door. A haggard old woman opened it. The housekeeper. She told them the priest was not at home; he was officiating at a funeral in the next village. But if they wished to wait... She took them to a low but spacious room, whose ceiling rested on thick, blackened beams. The two girls sat down on a black chest by the door and waited motionless. The priest's reception room was stark: there were no paintings or icons on the whitewashed walls, only a cross of black wood on the wall at the back and a thick leather-bound Bible on the large table in the middle.

Evening had fallen by the time he arrived, weary and dusty from the road. He took fright when he saw the two girls waiting for him.

'Has something happened at home, children?'

Rumours of what was happening had reached even the ears of Father Ignatius.

'Mama... Mama lied to us,' blurted Theodora, and large tear-drops welled in her eyes. 'She's a Jew...'

The priest remained rooted to the spot in amazement. Scenes flashed before his eyes, scenes that now took on a completely different meaning. He pictured Hanna sitting in the front pew of the church next to her husband, listening to the Sunday sermon, pale, tense, often perplexed. He remembered her blue, questioning eyes, her silences, her timid, frightened curiosity when he spoke of matters ecclesiastical. He remembered her stooping over the pregnant woman who had been shot in the middle of the street, in broad daylight. And only now did he understand that strange, unprecedented, upside-down confession of hers, which still rang in his ears, the fervent, desperate whisper in which she had said:

'I have not stolen!

'I have not killed!

'I have not lied or borne false witness!

'I have not coveted another's goods or envied another's happiness!

'I have not sinned in thought or deed before God or man!

'I have not blasphemed or gossiped or spoken ill of anybody!
'I have not done anybody harm!
'I have not wished anybody ill!
'I have not been faithless!
'I have not broken my word before God or man!
'Why then? Why then am I punished by God?'

The priest looked at the two girls, who with inflamed, tearful eyes were waiting for him to speak. Never had such a thing happened to him. Father Ignatius sensed that what he was about to say and do would have a lasting effect on the delicate souls of those children, would be incomparably more important than any mass or sermon. He considered for a while and then softly said: 'No, children, your mother did not lie! Did you ever ask her anything and she did not answer? No, she never lied to you… Perhaps the world, perhaps life lied to her.'

The priest fell to thinking. The girls looked at him in bewilderment, unable to understand. Father Ignatius went on: 'Do not forget that St Mary, the mother of Christ, was a Jew. And she suffered greatly, very greatly for her son. For all the children in the world. And your mother has suffered greatly, very greatly. You should go to her. She needs you, she needs her children. And you need your mother…'

Father Ignatius stood up from the table. He put on his wide-brimmed black hat, he took the girls by the hand, one to his right, one to his left, and he set off. They crossed the churchyard, they walked the length of the main street, dimly lit by flickering yellow electric bulbs, and finally reached the house. At the gate, the priest let go of the girls' hands and urged them: 'Go now, children! She is waiting for you.'

And he watched until they had crossed the front garden, until they had entered the house and closed the door behind them.

Hanna heard footsteps and quickly came out of the larder. She embraced the girls in silence.

'Where have you been, children? I looked for you everywhere. I thought I would lose my mind.'

Theodora remained silent. But Evuni hugged her mother and told her everything that nice old priest had said.

After a long moment, Hanna said: 'The three of us will stay together! They'll never break us apart, will they, girls?' Seeing a flicker of fear in the girls' eyes, she quickly added, 'And Daddy will come to see us, whenever he likes…'

She knew she had not answered their unspoken question, but she had no other answer. At least not for the moment. Perhaps time would better answer that question.

Hanna took the girls by the hand and they went into the bedroom. She put them to bed as she used to do when they were little, very little.

'Sleep tight!'

'Goodnight, Mama!'

The mother listened to the rhythmic breathing of her children; they had fallen asleep. Overcome by exhaustion, she curled up on Evuni's bed, by the little girl's feet, and fell into a sleep as grey and heavy as lead, an opaque, dreamless sleep.

When she awoke the next morning, her first thought was the same as her last thought before sleep felled her: Her girls had been lost and then miraculously found. She looked at Evuni. The little girl was sleeping peacefully and a serene smile trembled on her lips. She must be dreaming something nice. Hanna kissed her softly on the forehead. She then turned her gaze to Dora's bed. It was empty. On the bedside table there was a letter, in the girl's tidy, calligraphic hand.

'Dear Mama, I can't stay here any longer. I can't be anything other than what I am. I don't know what to tell my friends. And I don't know what to tell Vladi. He won't ask me and I won't tell him anything, and one fine day he'll think I've lied to him. Maybe nobody will ask me, and I'll feel like a liar. I'm going away to a town where nobody knows me, where I don't know anybody. Don't be afraid, Mama, I'm grown-up enough to find a job. I'll work somewhere and carry on with my studies. And maybe one day I'll come back to you. And to Daddy. I'll come home…'

Hanna sent for Theodor, who had spent the night in his office at the farm, lying on an old couch with broken springs, tossing and turning, unable to sleep. He came as fast as he could. Hanna showed him the letter. They talked like two strangers, who nonetheless had something in common, something that bound them together whether they liked it or not. They had to look for Dora, find out where she was, what she was doing… But ultimately, neither of them knew what to do; it was as if they had been struck senseless. They had always thought they knew their own children, but it turned out that they had no idea what was going on in their minds…

In the days that followed, Hanna, hand in hand with Evuni, whom she took with her everywhere, as if fearful of losing her, went to see Dr Halinski and his wife Margareta. She bid them farewell and asked them to inform her immediately if they heard any news of her elder daughter. She also went to see Thaddeus Andruschka the notary and his wife Elvira, making the same request. She spoke to Auntie Angela, the qualified midwife, who came to her every day to keep her company and bring her news from the village and surrounding area, news that interested Hanna not one whit. Hanna asked all her neighbours, both close and distant, to tell her elder daughter Theodora to go to her mother should she return. Finally, she went to say goodbye to Father Ignatius. But even though she had rehearsed what she would say dozens of times, when she came face to face with him, she was unable to utter a single word.

And without waiting for the divorce to be pronounced, Hanna left the village where she had lived happily and unhappily. It seemed to her now that she had simply existed there, nothing more. With her little daughter Evuni, she moved back to the town of her birth.

Resuming her maiden name, Hanna Kamin, she rented a furnished room and found a job in an office. Holding Evuni by the hand, once only did she walk down the street of her childhood. She showed the little girl the house where she had lived, she told her of her grandparents, her mother Riva and her father David Kamin, the Friday evening candles to greet Queen Sabbath, the thick, moth-eaten, leather-bound books from which David Kamin used to read to her on Saturday afternoons. 'Every love that depends on a thing perishes along with the thing.' The members of the Great Assembly said: 'Be moderate and prudent, do not be hasty to pass judgement.' And she told her of that dog-eared book with the strange title, *Tzeena Ureena*, 'Let Us Go Out, Let Us See,' from which her mother used to read her all those strange parables, about cities destroyed for the slightest thing, because of a cock or a hen, or because of a cart shaft, or because of a guest insulted at a feast, and ultimately because people no longer knew how to get along… Cities destroyed, but not forgotten, cities now rebuilt, which would last forever and ever through the power of love and mutual understanding…

Hanna also walked hand in hand with Evuni past her father's clock repair shop. Instead of the tall, thin clockmaker, she found a short, bald man. The clock was no longer there either: the clock with its enamelled face and elongated Roman numerals, with its sun-like brass pendulum and its turreted ebony case, by which David Kamin used to set the time of all the timepieces he repaired.

A light patch on the grey wall marked the place where the clock had once hung.

In her small office at the town's fruit cannery, Hanna spent eight hours a day, registering incoming mail, distributing letters to the various departments, writing addresses on envelopes and gluing stamps. Newspapers also arrived in the post and she leafed through them without any great interest. No longer did she have any expectations in life, but even so, she was waiting for something. Specifically, she was waiting for news from her eldest daughter Theodora. Sooner or later she would come back to her. At the bottom of her heart, she could not help but agree with her: She too felt like going some place far away, where nobody knew her, where nobody knew about her past life, where she could finally be herself once more, the person she used to be, or the person she ought to have been but had not been able to become. She was waiting for news from Dora or about Dora. She was also waiting for something else, something vague, indistinct, but the days passed and nothing arrived. One day, a registered letter arrived from engineer Theodor Bistricki, addressed to her, but with the words 'For Evuni' written in small, discreet letters on the envelope. With the same discreetness, she refused receipt of the registered letter. The postman wrote on the envelope in ink pencil: 'Addressee refuses receipt.' From her wages, she could afford to keep herself and her daughter, and for the time being, she needed nothing more.

Hanna leafed through the newspapers, she read the headlines, but the only column that interested her was titled 'Relatives seeking relatives.' Yes, even years after the end of the war, people were still looking for relatives, friends, acquaintances who had been scattered all over the world. No matter how strange it might seem, reading those unfamiliar names, sought by other unfamiliar names, soothed her, it made her not feel so alone. Until the day when names all too familiar leapt out at her from the smooth page of newsprint, as if the tiny black letters had been carved in relief. Her heart thudding, Hanna read: 'Esther Kamin seeks her niece Hanna. Maybe she hasn't forgotten the rag doll. Please send any information about her to this address…'

Yes, it was Esther Kamin, her Aunt Esta, the flighty family adventuress, who instead of making a 'good match' had run off with a young student as crazy as she was… Although she was a skilled seamstress and could have set up her own salon de mode, she had decided to learn how to work the land instead and went off to break stony ground that had long lain fallow. Even the way the announcement was worded betrayed that madcap girl… Good God, how could she have forgotten that comical rag doll, which used to make you want to laugh, what with its dress of red, blue, green and yellow patches, its pink cap sewn onto its head so that you could never take it off, even when you put it to bed in its little cot… And the doll's pink face, its eyes drawn with ink pencil dipped in water: two big dots, its nose: a vertical line, its mouth: a horizontal line.

And all of a sudden it struck her that that mute, comical doll was in fact she herself… a Hanna with a cloth face, a cloth heart, coddled, loved, and then mislaid, lost in the big, wide world…

And then found once more…

Hanna found herself weeping in the small, narrow post room. Warm, silent, soothing tears…

The two of them were sitting at the small round table in the restaurant of the large international airport. Hanna's coffee cup was long since empty, likewise Evuni's large glass of pink and green raspberry and pineapple ice cream. The little girl picked up the glass and tilted it, like a drunkard, trying to drain the last drop of melted ice cream.

'Evuni, what are you doing?' her mother gently scolded her.

It all seemed like a dream, a hallucination from which she had barely awoken. The only reality was the empty coffee cup in front of her, the child playing with the glass from which she had now licked every last drop of ice cream, the airport, the people coming and going, the luggage, the large silver aeroplanes visible through the wall of glass, landing on the white cement strips, elegantly taking off before vanishing into the distance, the metallic, slightly distorted voice of the loudspeaker: 'Flight 713 will be taking off in ten minutes. Passengers are requested to go to gate three.'

'Come on, Evuni, let's go!'

Hanna took the little girl's arm and they left.

Ludovic Bruckstein

ME: An Unabridged Autobiographical Novel

The time has definitely come for me to write my autobiography. To write down all the interesting things in my life. No matter how many hefty tomes it will fill. The world, posterity need to know everything...

Well, let me begin with the fact that I was born. Of good parents. A good father and a good mother. Not better than other parents, although for a long time I believed they were. That's because I have never been the child of other parents. But even so, the more deeply I think about it, the more certain I am that they were good parents. I remember that when my aunts used to tease me and ask, "Which do you love the most, your mother or your father," I always unhesitatingly answered, "I love both the same."

In time I grew up, with the result that on every birthday I became a year older. I went to primary, secondary and upper schools, and sometimes I did well, sometimes poorly. I had good teachers and mediocre teachers. I learned a large number of things, both useful and useless.

I was unlucky with women. Because they didn't want to be the way I imagined they should be. I also was fairly lucky with women. I had ideals and illusions, I had disappointments and was dealt slaps in the face both stinging and soft. I even came a step away from suicide, but I didn't take that step.

I travelled the world, to a moderate extent. I saw museums, temples, ruins, hotels, and beautiful air stewardesses.

I have been through a major, global war and two minor, regional wars, seven concentration and forced labour camps, a flood, two minor earthquakes, three childhood diseases, a number of spiritual crises, and I am still alive. Why? I don't know.

I have earned my daily bread doing various kinds of work and in various jobs. I am married. I have a son who lives his own life.

I never rode Rosinante, because I have never had a horse. Not that I know how to ride. Nor did I ever tilt at windmills, because no windmill has ever barred my way. Nor am I skilled in the ways of war.

And . . . what else might I add? Nothing.

1985

'(…) Bruckstein understood that his true vocation was to be a storyteller, and he also understood that as a storyteller, he could find complete fulfilment only by being part of a tradition, by continuing a specifically Jewish tradition, by innovating, but within this tradition, and with the air of not doing so. And thus, he accepted the condition of the *maggid*. (…) This is how Bruckstein remains in our minds: a true *maggid*, who seems to have a single purpose in life: that of making us understand the beauty of Hassidic spirituality. (…) for him writing was not a game, or a progression, or a means of gaining a more advantageous social position. For him writing was something essential, something holy, a *mitzva*, which he had to fulfil no matter what. Writing engaged the whole of his being. He could not live without writing, without communicating with his fellow men, to enrich their lives, to make their lives more beautiful. He wrote for as long as he lived. In the throes of writing. He died a hero's death, which is to say, writing, the same as Yaakov the Maggid must have died, telling the wonderful deeds of the Baal Shem Tov.'

Eugen Luca, *Viața noastră*, 12 August 1988

'(...) Ludovic Bruckstein was a singular figure of his time. He wished to combine Judaism with the revolutionary ideals of the post-war years. From this combination arose a socialist Hassid, not dissimilar to the "leftist" Catholic priests of Latin America, who came down from the pulpit to demonstrate for social reform. (...) He had a vocation for isolation, at every level. (...) It is here that we find the key to Ludovic Bruckstein: an uninterrupted contract with his own authenticity. He had the strength not to break with himself, he refused to pretend to be the kind of writer he was unsuited to be; he perfectly embodied the slogan of the ancient Greeks: "Know thyself."

Later, having emigrated to Israel in 1972, he was to act in the same way (...) the themes of the texts written in Tel Aviv are the same as those written in Bucharest. (...)'

Al. Mirodan, *Dicționar neconvențional al scriitorilor de limbă română*, Tel Aviv, 1986

First published in 2019 by
Istros Books
London, United Kingdom www.istrosbooks.com

Copyright © Estate of Ludovic Bruckstein, 2019

First published as
Scorbura, Panopticum, Tel Aviv, 1989
Păpușa de cîrpă, Panopticum, Tel Aviv, 1973

The right of Ludovic Bruckstein, to be identified as the author of this work has been asserted in accordance with the Copyright, Designs and Patents Act, 1988

Translation © Alistair Ian Blyth

Typesetting: Davor Pukljak, www.frontispis.hr
Illustrations: Alfred M. Bruckstein
Cover picture of L. Bruckstein taken by Rita Bruckstein, 1987

ISBN: 978-1-912545-31-5

The publishers would like to express their thanks for the financial support that made the publication of this book possible:
The Prodan Romanian Cultural Foundation
Arts Council England

PRODAN ROMANIAN
CULTURAL FOUNDATION

Lightning Source UK Ltd.
Milton Keynes UK
UKHW010605080819
347613UK00002B/45/P